CW01638504

The Inbetween People

Emma McEvoy

To Jacqui,
with best wishes

ASHGROVE PUBLISHING
London

For my parents, Gerard and Margaret McEvoy

And, for my Auntie Una, who very much wanted to read this book

Acknowledgements

I'd like to thank Yvonne Cassidy, who first asked me if I'd go to Listowel.

Special thanks to the following people I met in various workshops along the way, at both Listowel Writers Week and the West Cork Literary Festival: Bernie Furlong, Ciara Geraghty, Stephen Byrne, Dominic Bennett, Susan Browne, Ger Jennings, Christina Park, Mark Ryan, Gerard Donovan, Grainne Hayes, Donal O'Sullivan, Kathleen Murray, Christine Peterson, Carol Brick and Eileen Kavanagh. Thanks to all of you for your encouragement at various stages of the writing of this novel.

I would like to thank my agent, David Forrer, for all of the guidance, enthusiasm and help.

Thanks to Marty and Judith Shepard at The Permanent Press for being such a pleasure to work with.

I want to thank my friend Orla Dempsey for always being a good listener and for being such a great support in different ways.

I'd also like to thank Kirsty Mclachlan for all of the encouragement she gave me with regards to this novel.

I would like to particularly thank Michael Collins who read an early draft of this book and provided invaluable support and guidance at many different stages. Thanks for introducing me to my agent, and for always believing in this novel. Writing a novel, particularly a first novel, is lonely at times. Thanks for making it less lonely.

Thanks also to my family: my parents; my sister and brother who are always so supportive.

Special thanks to my husband, Efi Feldshtein, for all of the help, support and cooked dinners, and to my son Cian for helping and supporting in so many ways.

Lastly, special thanks to my dog Barkley, for his uncomplicated company while I write.

Hummingbird

by Raymond Carver

Suppose I say summer,
write the word "hummingbird,"
put it in an envelope,
take it down the hill
to the box. When you open
my letter you will recall
those days and how much,
just how much, I love you.

Chapter One

Ancient Egyptians believed they were gods of the underworld, and that their nightly howls were the haunting songs of the dead.

I believe it too. On nights like this when I sense Saleem's presence, hot nights when I can smell my own sweat, and the cry of the jackal is all around me. I hear his voice at times, the Hebrew words awkward upon his tongue. His voice finds me even here.

It's always the same when he comes: I get out of bed, fumble through the blackness until the edge of the desk cuts against my thigh. The desk is the one luxury I have here. The stone floor is cool against my bare feet. I grope for the candle, warm and soft in the heat of the night. I strike a match. I sit. The candle flickers through the darkness, a thin yellow glow, just enough light to write with.

My name is Avi Goldberg. I am twenty-five. I am in military prison because I am refusing to serve my country. I should be in Gaza now, seeing out my army service. Instead I am here. This is the most interesting fact to note about my life to date.

I write, I write through the hours of darkness, until it becomes less dense, the jackals retreat into the last shadows of the night. A gleam of light appears in the east, a halo in the darkness. If there is such a thing as redemption it comes at this time, it is the first light in the morning sky.

I am writing this for you, Saleem. I am writing about us, about how I loved you and how I killed you. I write. The pen moves to and fro.

Chapter Two

She slams her keys down on the table so that the woman at the next cubicle jumps and at least three couples turn to stare at us. Her smell comes to me through the wire gauze, the smell of lemon and sunshine.

It's terrible here, she says. A flake of plaster floats down from the ceiling and lands on her wrist. She glances at it, then brushes it away.

It's not so bad, I say. You get used to it.

It's far worse than I thought it would be, she says. Her eyes search my face, resting on my lips. And you still have three weeks left here.

I stare at her hands. The skin is smooth and her nails are scarlet. And I know that it is important she looks her best for this.

I'm sorry I didn't come to see you off, she says. I was hoping you'd change your mind. It's ridiculous that you're here in prison. By choice.

It's right that I'm here, I say. I've felt that since I arrived.

She looks around, picks up her keys again. She presses them hard against her lower lip so that it turns white. There is a thin line of sweat across her forehead. She says, I need you to get me out of here. I need to get out of this country soon.

I don't speak. She isn't looking at me, she is looking towards the open window.

They want me to marry Karim, she says.

Karim. Saleem's brother.

Have they said that?

Yes, she says. We will marry on the sixteenth of December. I must be gone by then. She turns to look at the woman in the cubicle next to us, the woman is leaning towards the soldier she is visiting, talking in low, even tones.

Avi, I can't marry Karim, she says. She leans towards me, her voice low. I need you to help me. The words dart away from her, thin, desperate.

Can nobody else help you?

You know there is nobody, she says.

Nobody?

You, Avi.

I shrug. What can I do about it, I say.

I've thought about this, she says, I know exactly what I have to do. She places her hand against her temple, begins to fan her face. There are no other options, she says. There is only you.

I light a cigarette.

For a time after he died I thought maybe they would send me home, she says, that's why I didn't come to you sooner. She wipes her hand along her forehead and the sweat streaks outwards, like a web. That would have been the end, she says; but they weren't happy to do that, my father is dead and I have no brother to act as my guardian. Her eyes are blurred and she tosses her head.

I place the cigarette against my lips. I know what this is costing her, I know how it is in her community.

I'm useless to anyone, she says. She presses her hands

hard against the wooden frame in front of her, her knuckles are very white. She looks straight at me, as if her black eyes can force me to understand.

I flick the ash from my cigarette, it falls on the stone floor. I grind it into the dust with the sole of my shoe. She is not a virgin, no one else in her community will marry her now; she is somebody else's past, the responsibility of her dead husband's family. I pull hard on my cigarette, I know why she is here.

I have a plan, she says.

It better be good, I say. Still, it won't take account of –

Saleem's dead, she says. There's no point bringing him up. He can't change anything for me now.

Her eyes are empty, resting on the clock above my head. I can hear it ticking. She looks away from the clock, back at me, moves her face closer to the gauze. She takes a tissue from her bag.

It's so hot here, she says. I hate this time of year when everything is full of dust. She wipes the sweat off her forehead with the tissue, rolls it between her palms. The warden said I don't have long, she says. He said ten minutes. I need to ask you something. Don't answer straight away. Think about it. Like you promised on the beach.

I can do that, I say.

Good, she says. She smiles. You take that time.

The dust of November is on her face. She rubs her fingers against her face, caressing the dust, and when she takes her hand away there is a streak of mascara down her cheek. For the first time I notice that she is wearing makeup, and I smile at her clumsy attempts to beautify herself. I imagine her applying it in the car, on a white chalk mountain road, and I know that no trace of it will remain when she returns to her village at nightfall.

I close my eyes. I hear her voice coming to me.

Your father was English. You have a right to a British passport. Apply for it. While you're here, fill out the papers and send them off. She pushes a bundle of papers towards me under the gauze. Here are the papers. When your time here is up, go straight to the airport. I'll be there with the tickets. We'll leave the same night.

She waits for me to speak.

You will be released on the twenty-ninth of November, she says. That is the date, isn't it?

I nod.

I've thought it all through, she says. All of it. It's a Thursday. They think I'm in class on Thursdays. That's how I'm here now. By the time they notice I'm gone we'll be on the way to England. We'll get married so that I'll be legal. We'll both work, have money maybe for the first time in our lives. She falters, hesitates, recovers, the words come again. We'll settle somewhere nice, in a little house with a garden. I'll take your name. They'll never find me.

And where exactly will you work? I say.

I'll work anywhere.

Do you think you'd be happy living with me?

What? She hesitates. Of course.

She doesn't look at me when she says this. There is silence then and the voices of the couple in the next cubicle come to us. The woman's voice is raised, the man's soothing.

I met her husband, Saleem, on a beach by a lake on a July

day. I'd been to the lake before, and there was a specific beach in my mind that day, a deserted place. I had a blinding headache that afternoon, so that every side track appeared the same. And as I drove through the reeds, on and on, it seemed like I was going further away from the water and that I'd never find a beach, but then there was one before me, rising out of the rushes, seemingly deserted and very beautiful; small and isolated, reflecting the stillness of that July afternoon.

I got out of the car and stood there, examining the beach with the sun on my back.

I resented the fact that he came up behind me and I didn't hear him. Sometimes I still resent it, our very introduction never went away. He had a quiet way of moving, as if the world he walked in was very fragile, and everything he touched was brittle.

He tapped me on the back, and when I turned to face him he smiled. I later came to know that smile, but I read then that this was his beach and I was intruding though he was too courteous to say so.

Sorry, I said.

He shrugged and pointed to his fishing line. Then he sat on a rock and began to fish. I understood what he meant and I wouldn't have parked there had I known he was already on the beach, but part of me wanted to stay, the same part that was annoyed at him creeping up behind me.

He was a natural fisherman, I saw it straight away. He stood on a black rock, his shirt stuck to his body, and I remained there for some time watching him catch small silver fish, one after the other. In the end he turned to face me.

I'm Saleem, he said.

I smiled at him, though I didn't feel it, not then, and I told him my name, Avi, before I plunged into the water. It was cold, so cold, after the heat of the afternoon, and I swam until the heat was gone and I no longer felt the glare from the sky; and when I came out he was still sitting on the rock. I'd decided I was going to stay.

I took a mattress from the car and lay down in the shade of the rushes. I was tired for I'd just completed my compulsory annual army-reserve service. I slept.

Sometimes here, when I need to sleep, I imagine that I am there on that beach, sleeping, and he is fishing, and I can hear the ripple of the water and the thud of the silver fish landing on the black rock. I feel the heat of the sun, and my weariness that day, and I sleep.

*

Saleem would want you to take me there.

I open my eyes and Sahar is in front of me, her hair black against the wire gauze. There is triumph in her eyes, and something else that I don't care to analyse, a cunning that I'd glimpsed in her before.

I'm not sure, I say.

She drops the keys onto the table. Why are you making this so difficult? she says. You said you'd give it some thought. Do you really think he'd want me to marry Karim, to be a prisoner in the home he created for me? Didn't you know him at all? Her voice is raised.

My time is nearly up, she says. She nods towards Zaki, the warden. He will come soon, she says. Can you think about it, Avi?

Will you stay with me? I say.

What?

Will you stay with me? After you get your citizenship. Will you stay with me?

Of course.

How do I know you don't have other plans? How do I know you'll stay? I'm not Saleem.

The woman in the next cubicle is sobbing now. Please do your army service, she says. Can't you imagine what people will say? Have you thought about the children? I haven't told anyone you're here. Please stop this ridiculous farce. The man is uncomfortable, he glances at me, then they lean closer and whisper, her hair almost falling into his face.

Sahar moves her foot towards a cockroach. It is quiet, immobile, placed exactly between our two sets of feet. I'll stay, she says. You have to trust me. You do this for me, Avi. You do this for me and I'll never leave. Where else would I go, she says?

I light another cigarette. I know something about the dead, something she does not yet know, I know how they cling on and somehow remain, how they refuse to leave. I shrug. Come next week, I say. Come next visiting day. I'll give you the answer then.

She presses her face up against the wire gauze that separates us, reaches under it and squeezes my hand.

Thanks, she says. Thanks for thinking about it. Zaki the warden is moving towards us. She stands in front of me, next week, she says, I'll come again. You can tell me then. She clutches at the gauze, you must tell me then, she says.

Are you done? Zaki says.

She nods but turns away from him. Avi, she says, her voice is urgent, you must apply for the passport this week, no matter what. I've given you all the papers you need for a successful application. Even if you later decide you won't come.

Zaki reaches his hand out to her elbow, come, he says, and she turns to him, she pushes her hair back from her face. She walks with him, towards the open doorway, the sunlit afternoon; the sun has reached inside and is casting narrow flames of light across the floor. She walks into the sunlight and for a time after she has gone, it seems that I can still see her shadow in the doorway.

*

My mother left in July. Father told me a little about that day, years later, that it was hot, the hottest day that year. When she woke that morning she cried and begged him to take her to England. He explained to her that he could not leave because there was work to be done on the kibbutz where they lived, and he believed in that work and in the future, not just for him he said, but for the country, for future generations.

It's not about individual happiness, he said. It's about the collective happiness of the community. You must remember that.

When he came home that evening there was a note on the table. It said that she had fallen in love with a Dutch man, a man who came to volunteer to work on the kibbutz for six months. He was bringing her to Holland. She was sick of living in the countryside on a kibbutz, tired of everyone knowing her business, tired of the heat and the sweat. She didn't want to leave, she would have stayed with us if it was possible, if we could have left too. She never wanted to see another field, nor an orchard, not even an ear of corn ripening in the sunshine. She wanted to concentrate on her art, to see more of the world. Take care of my Avi, it said.

I asked him once if I could see the letter, but he said that he hadn't kept it. He said, you're too young to remember. You were only five.

But I remembered her: her smell of summer flowers, the way her hair blew across her face on windy days. And her laugh, a tingly sound that came from the very heart of her. I waited for her for years – my eyes wandering to doorways at my birthday parties, at Rosh Hashanah, Passover and all our holidays – because for a long time I believed she would come home, walk through one of those doorways, into one of those rooms, home to me. And at night, just before I slept, I would feel her lips kissing my eyelids. Sometimes even now I feel her breath on my skin.

*

Zaki, the warden, is coming for me. I stand to meet him and I walk away from that room and I don't look back. The sobbing of the other woman follows me through the grey windowless corridor, all the way back to my empty cell.

Chapter Three

All stories have a beginning, you said. And that is not necessarily the obvious beginning. It's not always like David Copperfield, you said, things don't always have to begin at the very beginning.

And so Saleem, just as once – when you asked me to tell you my story – I instinctively knew that it began with Mother leaving, so I know where your story begins: it is another July day, hot, but it's always hot here in July. You are beside your grandmother on the backseat of your uncle Sabri's minivan, on the way to Safsaf for the first time, forehead pressed against the window, seeing nothing new, only the curved white road before you, the trees laden with the dust of summer. Safsaf is part of your life, mentioned always with reverence and sadness, spoken of in heavy lifeless tones.

You imagined that Safsaf was far away, perhaps across the ocean, a place that knew snow intimately, somewhere that smelt of the sea. Never a short drive away, another part of these same mountains of white stone and summer dust where you've always lived.

We're here, says uncle Sabri. You scramble out of the car into the heavy heat of July, and all of Galilee glimmers below you, a great shimmering mass of burnished stone. Grandmother remains motionless, rocking to and fro against the seat. Uncle Sabri points to the house, an enormous cold structure behind you. It's this one, isn't it?

She nods, but does not raise her head.

Is this the house? you ask.

In one motion, she moves from the minivan over to the black gate that is speckled with rust. She fumbles with it, her thin frame struggling to open it. Her eyes rest on you. Don't you recognise this house child? Haven't you been paying attention all these years? Haven't I told you all about his house? She dusts you down, smoothes your hair, her hand rough, trembling. Stand up straight, she says.

It is the hottest part of the afternoon, you follow her into the garden, the branches of an olive tree are swaying. She walks toward the house, clawing your arm and pulling you after her. She breathes deeply, her nostrils expanding and contracting like a fish. The place seems to fill her completely. It's good air, she says.

You are frightened by her intensity, the way her fingers grasp at your wrist. Tighter, tighter. You want to go home. This isn't home, this is nothing.

She reaches the front the door, drops your arm, fondles the wood with her bare hands, reaches out and smells it. She places her cheek against it, sighs a deep sigh, stands back, inhales the mountain air. She begins to walk around the house, clutching your arm again, gazes down at the distant villages below, crouches down and scratches at the dry earth, turns her face up to the sun. She begins to cry. Blindly she clutches the leaf of a lemon geranium, and the smell is all around you. My garden, she says.

She rises to her feet, continues to clutch at your wrist, kneading your flesh, leading you back towards the great wooden door. You want to turn around and run home, this place is nothing to you, this dark staring house, it frightens you how being here moves her. Uncle Sabri hammers on the door, shattering the stillness of the July afternoon.

The door opens to a woman. You don't know her age, you always think of her as thirty-five. Her face stays with you for years, her cream skin, the clean smell of soap. She is startled, disturbed, as if she has been sleeping. She rubs at her eyes and steps out past the doorway, dragging the door closed behind her. She waits for one of you to speak, one eyebrow raised slightly.

Can I help you? she asks.

Your grandmother's mouth moves but she doesn't speak.

Uncle Sabri steps forward towards her. This woman used to live in this house, he says. She wanted to come back and see it again. She feels she is not well and she wants to see it. She lives somewhere else now, not too far from here. He gestures with his hand towards the distant villages.

The Jewish woman digests this. She frowns at first and her eyes close a little. She turns to your grandmother. You are welcome, she says.

Your grandmother nods in her direction, her black eyes flaring.

The woman pushes the door open behind her, arms out.

You enter. It is dark after the bright heat outside. You can't see much but it smells musty, as if no one lives there at all, as if this house is too big for this little woman. Your grandmother moves towards an oak table, reaches out and fondles the polished wood.

Tea, the Israeli woman says. Tea with mint?

Nobody answers.

Her eyes rest on you. And for you? she says. For you some Coca-Cola. Come with me. She holds out her hand to you and you go with her, through a dark hallway and into a kitchen that is filled with sunlight. She takes a tray of ice cubes from the freezer and places three square cubes in a glass. She fills the glass with Coca-Cola and thrusts it in your direction. It bubbles and fizzes in front of you. You stare at the brown bubbles as she fills the kettle.

I bought this house, she says. I bought it with my husband ten years ago. She reaches her hand up to her eyes, her face startled, as if surprised that she has lived in the house for ten years. We'll make the tea, she says.

You sip the Coca-Cola. It is cold and sugary. You move to the door and stand looking down into the garden. She comes and stands behind you.

It's got a great view, she says. I like this house. It was a man I bought it from. A German. He'd had enough of this country, decided to go home.

You don't answer. She seems to be apologising, for what you are not sure.

I knew it used to belong to the Arabs, she says, but I didn't realise you were still in the country. Come out to the garden, she says, we need to pick mint for the tea. Her bare feet nestle into the grass as she bends down to pick the mint. The smell of it comes to you, and one of her breasts becomes almost wholly visible as she leans towards the plants. She places the leaves in your hands. It's good mint, she says.

She asks you to carry the glasses through to your grandmother and uncle Sabri. Your grandmother is still standing in the same place, in front of the heavy wooden table.

That table was here, the woman says. It was here when I bought it.

It wasn't for sale, your grandmother replies. We never sold it.

Uncle Sabri goes out of the house into the garden, lights a cigarette. You see him through the window, kicking a stone, walking in an exact square, wiping the sweat from his brow. Your grandmother reaches out and strokes a vase that rests on the table.

The Israeli woman leaves you in front of the table and returns with a plate of biscuits. She pours three glasses of mint tea and sits, watching the two of you in front of the table. Your grandmother takes a sip from her glass, and sits down on the patterned couch facing the Israeli woman. You knock on the window, Uncle Sabri turns, you point towards the tea, but he shakes his head, raises his cigarette to his lips.

That vase on the table, your grandmother says. She looks the woman in the eye. That was my mother's, his great grandmother's. She points at you. That vase is ours, she says. It does not belong to you.

The Israeli woman lights a cigarette. She walks across the room towards your grandmother. Please take it, she says, take it from this house. I bought this house and it was here when I bought it. I just left it there because it was pretty on the table, and it looked like it belonged there.

That's because it did, says your grandmother.

I've never used it, the Israeli woman says. Please take it.

No, she says. No. I won't remove it from this house. It belongs here.

Do you want to look around the house, the Israeli woman says.

No, she says. I thought I did, but now that I'm here I don't want to after all. I see it's just the same anyhow. She finishes her tea, gets up from the couch, and stands in front of the great oak table. The view, she says, it is impossible to recreate a view. She turns to you. I think we should go now, she says. I just wanted to see it, that's all.

You leave the house, nobody addresses the Jewish woman. Grandmother walks slowly, one foot in front of the other, eyes fixed straight ahead. As you reach the minivan you feel someone clutching your shoulder. The Jewish woman.

Take it, she says. Her eyes are wide, panicked. I don't want it in my house, she says. She thrusts the vase at you. Please take it. It belongs to your family. It is just a small thing, something that I can give back to you. She is bending down, eyes staring into yours, her nails digging into the skin on your shoulder.

You avert your gaze. We don't want it.

Please, she says. Please. I want you to have it.

You take it, and the Jewish woman drifts back towards her home. The vase is cold, it fits perfectly in your hand. You sit in the minivan, and you hold it against your cheek. Later, when you are almost home, your grandmother notices it. Her eyes flare with anger.

She bought you, she hisses. She bought you with her low top and her big breasts. She reaches out and strikes you on the cheek. You reel back, tears sting the back of your eyes but you don't cry.

Because of you she has bought me too, she says. Her face is purple and her chin is flecked with spittle. She has bought us all, she has bought our family. That's what they do, these people, they buy us. One by one. She shakes her head, her eyes blaze at you. Is it not enough that she has my home. She strikes your cheek again. She cries then, great heaving sobs that shake the minvan. You finger the vase, and stare at it until you seem to become part of it.

That night you hold it against you as you sleep. It seems to fit, a part of you, part of the boy you were when you had a mother.

Chapter Four

I'm allowed one call per week. I dial her number and turn to the window, wipe away the dust with my sleeve. It's that dry wind outside again, the trees outside bow against it, exhausted now. I sit down and light a cigarette, run my hand through my hair.

She doesn't answer immediately. It rings and rings, and just as I am reaching to replace the receiver, I hear her voice.

Sahar, it's me, I say. I applied for a passport. They are sending me the forms. I speak through cracked lips.

Hello, she says.

Well, I say. Are you not pleased?

How are you? she says, her tone formal. How nice to hear from you.

David, the occupant of the cell opposite mine, is behind me now, waiting for his phone call. He jingles the change between his hands, shifts from foot to foot, takes out a cigarette, lights it, and the flame is hot against my nape.

Is someone there? I say.

I am as well as can be expected, thank you, she says.

David coughs behind me, a quiet cough – he smokes a lot of cigarettes in here. I can tell he's in no hurry, he doesn't mind listening.

Is it Karim? I say. Instinctively I know that Karim is there with her; I think of him and how Saleem disliked him, how he never fully admitted that but how I knew just the same.

She doesn't answer, but she takes a deep breath and there are tears in it.

Why is he there?

I told you, she says.

David leans towards the window, he wipes away more dust, exhales the smoke from his lungs towards it.

Come next week, I say. We'll make our plans then.

Thanks so much for calling, she says. It's so kind of you to remember Saleem.

I put the phone back on the receiver, stand looking at it, and then David is beside me jingling his change again, his cigarette between his lips.

That the Arab girl you were talking to? he asks, the one who comes to visit? Is she the reason you're here?

I turn away from him and walk towards Zaki. Can I go back now? I say, but no, he says, we'll wait for David, there's no point getting another warden to escort you. He won't be long.

He turns to David and points his keys at his eyes. Three minutes, he says, that's the rules.

Trust me, David says, three minutes is too long; my wife isn't too happy I'm in here. He smiles at me. I remember his wife, the woman with the raised voice on visiting day. I sit by the window and light a cigarette. I open the window and touch the outside air. I breathe it.

*

I never intended getting to know Saleem. I wasn't there long when I decided to leave the beach.

I was so tired that weekend, that was the problem. I slept there on the beach and when I awoke night had already descended. I groped around in the dark, shoving my belongings into my backpack, placed it on the backseat of the car, and when it was finally done I searched for Saleem to tell him I was leaving.

He had lit a fire, and was stoking it with shoots of the rushes that grew wild around the beach, the smoke from the fire curled up into the night sky above him, a swirling thick cloud in the heavy air. I saw his shadow across the beach, black in the light of the fire, and when I reached him I told him I'd decided to leave. He didn't look up from his task and we talked for a few moments before I turned away from him. Then there was pain everywhere and I was hopping on one foot, cursing the beach, myself, him, the bright hot heat of the fire, and the glass bottle that had been placed, broken and jagged, standing upright. I felt the glass break inside me, in the centre of my foot, and the blood leaving me, and the wetness of the sand below me.

Are you okay? He was beside me, gripping my shoulder.

I think so, I said, and he was pushing me to sit, turning my foot to the fire, examining the wound in the light from the flames.

Who leaves glass bottles lying around like that? It's bad, he said. It's a bad cut.

I'll be fine. Now it was numb, I felt nothing.

He ran to his car, rummaged in the back of it, while my foot was beginning to throb, a dull pain. He came back and went about cleaning it, using pliers to remove the individual shards of glass; then he bathed it in alcohol and bandaged it up. It's clean now, and I think I got all the glass out. But you can't drive today, or tomorrow either. You should probably see a doctor in the next few days, he said.

Where did you learn to do that? I asked.

Oh, that's nothing.

You had training for what you just did.

He turned towards me. Yes, I did actually, he said. I was a paramedic in the army.

You served?

Yes.

You chose to serve? Arab Israelis had a choice.

Yes, I chose to serve. He smiled. A lot of people serve in an army because they have principles, he said. Because they believe in a greater good, or in something at least. Sorry to disappoint you, but I don't have any principles. I don't care about any of it. I served just to annoy my grandmother.

Did it work?

He laughed. I thought I would get more reaction than that, he said. Yes, of course it worked. You didn't know my grandmother.

So I can't drive? I'm stuck here on this beach.

Yes, he said, I'm cooking fish now if you want some. He began to move around the fire again, and presently the smell of fish came through the air. A mosquito landed on my arm, and I slapped at it so hard I stung my flesh.

*

It is autumn now, or what passes for autumn here, and the evening air gets slightly cooler once the sun sinks in the sky. David is beside me.

That didn't go well, he said. You probably heard.

Sorry, I say, I wasn't listening.

My wife, he says, it's breaking her heart that I'm in here. She wants me to carry out my service. She told her family I'm here and they're upset about it.

We turn to look at Zaki, who is pacing up and down, talking on his mobile phone.

That girl, David says. Is she the reason you're in here?

I glance at him. He has ideals, believes in what he is doing, someone like my father would have been at that age. No, she's not, I say.

His hands are in his pockets, and he's groping for leaflets, pulling them out, thrusting them at me. They are full of statistics. There are lots of soldiers like us, he says. Conscientious objectors.

Is that what I am? I say.

He turns to regard Zaki, who is striding away from us, each stride an exact measure, the same as the last one. David thrusts a cigarette towards me. You know what you are, he says. And though you keep yourself to yourself and don't talk much, we appreciate you being here, we appreciate what you're doing. His lighter is in his hands and he lights my cigarette.

I look at him, a stocky man of average height, a strong jawline and striking blue eyes that hit me with the force of their integrity every time he looks at me.

We know it's not easy, he says. Almost one month, that's the sum of your time here. The time you should be in the Reserves. He reaches out and puts his hand on my arm. Why not make things easier on yourself. If you need to talk, you talk. I need to talk all the time, he says. My wife, he says, she cries about this, she finds it hard to understand. You should serve where you're told to serve, she says to me. She's never been to Gaza. He laughs. But we're a growing movement, he says. People are beginning to listen. He has another leaflet in his hand. This boy he says, this boy was eleven when he was shot. In Ramallah. Eleven. He points his cigarette at the picture.

I stare at the picture, I hold it in my hands.

Kids throw stones, he says, eleven-year-old boys throw stones. The greatest sign of strength an army can display is to show mercy, he says.

It's windy, I hear the cypress trees whisper outside the window.

Avi, he says, it's good to talk. We have meetings you know. We support each other, we're all in this together. We all appreciate it's not easy, and we know that everyone arrives at this point for different reasons. If you want to be part of things you talk to me; it doesn't matter if your ideals or reasons are not the same as mine. We are all here to help each other. We know that you are here because of her.

Zaki is coming towards us, he pushes his hands against our backs.

Time to go back, he says. You, he nods at David. You were four minutes on the phone. That's one minute off your next call. We notice these things, he says, don't think we don't notice.

When I am back in my cell, David calls out to me. Avi Goldberg, he says. Conscientious objector, he shouts.

The light has dimmed and suddenly night has descended. I lie on my bed for a time – I like the evenings in the desert, the bright light disappearing from the sky, the fingers of light that remain growing dimmer, darker, until night is upon me. The sun sets abruptly in the desert. For some minutes before it is swallowed by the night, it turns into a flaming fire, then it is gone. Night descends quickly, with little fanfare. I believe it is different elsewhere. Father told me of lingering twilights in England, a magical time between night and day, when the light is still in the day and the first stirring of darkness is creeping into the night. He told me of long, glorious sunsets, explosions of light across the sky, the slow descent of night. The darkness comes quickly here, closes in relentlessly, descends upon us completely and absolutely – that is the way of the desert.

Avi Goldberg, shouts another prisoner, we salute you.

Chapter Five

There is another beginning. Maybe I didn't begin at the beginning. It's hard to know; it's not as exact a science as you believed, finding a beginning.

You are Saleem, first born son of Talibah. I do not know her second name, you never told me. Talibah, who married at seventeen, had six children, all boys, and died, aged twenty-seven, in childbirth.

Being the first born son of Talibah means a lot: that you are first to lick the spoon when she makes her sweet biscuits, the ones that melt on your tongue; that you are the first she kisses goodbye in the morning when you line up to say goodbye before school; the last one she tucks into bed at night, the last one to feel her soft kiss and her whispered blessing. It means that you understand things the other boys don't, and that you get to do things they don't because you are the biggest. It means that you know her best because you know her longest, and it means that you have to protect her – that you are home that day, sitting on the stairs, the back stairs that nobody ever uses.

You are sitting on the back stairs, on the marble stone leading to her room. A new baby is on the way. You've watched her tummy growing and Grandmother says the baby will arrive soon. She isn't well, there is talk that this must be the last one.

She is suffering. You hear her moaning but you can't go

in; if they see you they will send you away somewhere to play for the day. Your knuckles are scratched and bleeding because you fought with your brother Karim when he threatened to tell your father of your plan to stay home. You tortured him into submission, but he got hold of your knuckles and scraped them along the concrete.

She calls out then and you want to answer her. You rise to answer, you stand up and walk towards the dark door. You know she lies inside in her great big bed, and you want to help her, bring her water, rub ice against her warm cheeks – something – but you sit back down again when you remember what will happen if your grandmother sees you.

The cries go on all afternoon, and you sit there frozen to the ground. After a while you creep down to the kitchen; it is deserted, so you open the fridge and start to eat cheese and olives. And then Grandmother appears and she is angry, very angry, her nostrils expand, opening and closing, and you stare at them.

Have you defied your father, she screams. Why you are not with the other children?

You don't answer because you don't know how to tell her about your mother and that you are frightened, and how you think that she and your father don't love your mother, don't really love her the way you do.

Go to your room, she says. We have enough going on here.

She takes your arm and pulls you up the stairs, into your room, nearer now to Mother and her moans. Nearer, nearer, so that all afternoon in the dead heat of August you lie on your bed trying to block your ears, but still hear her moans, deeper, deeper, until eventually there is silence, and then there is the piercing cry of a baby – your new brother. A mosquito is flying around your ears, leaving a whistling echo in its wake. But your mother is silent and you know she is gone, and you sleep then, deeply with no dreams, nothing but emptiness.

Chapter Six

Daniel Goldberg
October 26th, 1985

Dear Sareet,

It is late October now and the land is readying itself for winter. Perhaps you remember the Galilee at this time of year, and think of it sometimes, the way the hot wind blows, followed always by rain, the cooler days, welcome at first, until the evenings become too short to escape the fact that winter is upon us. Perhaps because I am a gardener I notice it more than most, regret the passing of the glorious summer displays the garden bequeaths us, and perhaps I panic more than other people at the suddenness of the short evenings. There is so much to be done, you see, and I notice that more and more each year. I detect autumn in peoples' eyes too, the notion that another cycle is almost complete. I used to see it in your eyes, how you hated the coming of winter, and you don't know how often I have smiled to myself at the irony that you live somewhere where winter is so much harder and colder than here.

I suppose I should explain why I am writing to you. I am writing because I am worried about our boy. It seems strange for me to use the word 'our' in this context because it is four years now since you were part of his life, yet it is meant as a generous gesture, since I admit I must be doing something wrong.

It seems to me that Avi spends too much time on his own. It is difficult for me to write this, and for some years I vowed that I would not approach you regarding issues with the boy, yet I realise now that I have run into problems. It may surprise you that you are the most obvious person to share this with. I would like to assure you at this point that I try to include Avi in all aspects of my life. Certainly, he walks my gardens with me every evening. I tell him about the plants, their life cycle, the most suitable growing conditions for each plant, the factors that will most adversely affect their growth (or certainly their display!) and what they can expect of us now that winter is approaching. He is always attentive, I can't fault him for that. He listens and he nods, and later if I ask him about it he remembers, and is able to tell me precisely what I said.

He is good at his lessons, his teachers tell me that he is never troublesome or rude, indeed he is most polite. He is well-mannered towards the other children, but he doesn't play with them, or mix with them too much, they say. He is a good boy, they wish every child was like him, their job would be so much easier. And yet there is a kind of unease there, I can't quite put my finger on it, but it is as if they can't understand him.

We have fun too. Last month I brought him to a new

water park that opened here in the Galilee. We travelled there during the holidays. There were long queues for each ride, I should have anticipated it as part of the autumn holidays we celebrate here in this country, yet we enjoyed it just the same. Once a month we go together to the cinema, and he always gets to choose the movie he would like to see the night before.

He kills creatures.

I mean insects. It took me some time to realise this. I didn't pay enough attention when I found several dead wasps and bees around the place, nothing strange except these had been sliced exactly in half, with a fine blade. Then there were the dead spiders, or parts of spiders with their legs laid out separately from their body, and their webs in neat balls beside them. After that there were the cockroaches, but I simply despise those creatures and I was not sorry to see them dead.

I ignored it until the dead butterflies, and for a long time I did not realise what they were. Small blobs of colour on the doorstep or on the grass, rolled up into an untidy ball. I kicked out at them several times, not comprehending what they were until one day I saw him approaching one of my jasmine plants (the one you requested I plant) on tiptoe. It was a bright day, not too far past midday, and I saw him, suspended in gravity, approaching my jasmine plant, creeping towards it, and then his hand, swiping out, fingers clawing the air, catching a yellow butterfly in mid-flight, enclosing it in the palm of his hand, squeezing his hand tighter and tighter, before opening it out, and staring at it, then wiping it in the grass, near the area where you liked to sit on summer evenings, and going indoors.

I inspected the mess for some time after he disappeared indoors. My thoughts at the time are similar to what they are now, which is why I am writing to you: I wonder if it is because of our situation, because of the fact that he lives here on this kibbutz, a family orientated place indeed, without his mother, you. He never complains, nor does he speak about our situation, nor about the fact that there is only he and I, and I thought he was developing nicely, and saw it as a small victory on my part, until I discovered this business with the butterflies and the other insects.

Therefore, I am writing to you, Sareet, to request that you have more contact with the boy, indeed I am asking you to write to him once a month, so that he feels loved and wanted. I know you have said in the past that one can't put a timeframe on these things, and that you and Avi have a bond that I don't understand, and that your soul is linked to his, and his to yours, but Avi has not heard from you in years, and frankly I don't see that he feels any kind of bond. I will admit that I was hoping that he would forget about you as the years pass, but clearly he hasn't because he asks me about you sometimes, where you are and what you are doing and if you will return one day, and really, now that we are running into difficulties the situation is completely unsatisfactory.

He needs you. A boy needs his mother, and he needs you now. He needs to hear from you Sareet. I will leave it in your hands for the moment, and I trust you will deal with this situation accordingly.

Daniel

Chapter Seven

Winter is coming. I am in the gardens, digging up lettuce. The sting has deserted the fiery Arabian wind, the bright hot intensity cooled by a breeze that drifts in from the west, spreading swirling clouds across the sky.

I have a wheelbarrow piled high with lettuces; my work here completed for the day, I sit and write.

Why don't you talk about that girl who comes to visit? says David.

I sit on the wall, drive my pen far into one of the cracks, as far as it will go, and watch him dig. He works hard, preparing the ground for the winter potatoes.

David, I say. Why don't you mind doing this menial work? What makes you think you should do it?

He doesn't answer, pauses for a single moment, smiles and continues digging. He discovers something in the soil, halts his work, picks it up, wipes the clay away. I watch him; there is something about him that is different from the other prisoners impounded in this place. His movements are moderate, quiet, and he seems taller in the confined gardens than he really is, his long face poised in concentration as he stares at what he holds in the palm of his hand.

A ring, he says. I wonder how long it's been here in the earth. Another soldier must have lost it. He holds it up to the light, though the clouds are cutting across the sun, then puts it in his pocket and starts to dig again.

He rests his foot on his rake, shakes the clay from his boots. I watch him; despite the fact that he is a stocky man, his movements are delicate. You know, he says, I could ask why you don't work, what the hell it is you are writing. I dig because there is nothing else to do here except the work they expect us to do. That's why I do it, I'm bored. I don't like doing nothing.

He puts his head in his hands and there are streaks of mud across his high forehead. I've never done nothing, he says. He looks at the sky. It's raining, he says. He unfolds his palms in front of him and touches the rain, stares at the drops that fall into his open hands. I know nothing about you, Avi, he says, nothing at all. I don't know what it is you are doing here, why that girl comes. You don't talk, you don't tell us anything. Part of being here is talking, people need a support network. We are only human.

He thrusts the rake into the earth. So why don't you work, Avi? Why don't you ever help out? Why do you sit on a wall while I dig? While I fill your wheelbarrow with lettuces to keep them happy? He points towards the building. Why do you need nobody here? The rake scrapes against a rock, he pushes his foot down on it, it is futile, the rake does not budge, but still he stands on it, driving it against the rock. The rain continues to fall, strengthening in intensity, great panes of water. The first rain, he says. I always love the first rain.

It is heavy now, and I hold out my hands to it, summer is gone in that instant.

Why are you here, Avi? he says. Everybody's story is equally important. You must understand that. Nobody here is more important than anyone else, nobody has something to say that is more important than what you have to say. Everybody came here for a reason and each individual circumstance is equally valid.

*

I couldn't sleep the night I met Saleem, my foot was throbbing and I'd slept too late that afternoon. For a time I tried, I lay in the heat; but my foot ached, and the mosquitoes whistled in my ears and landed on my skin until eventually I rose and limped to the fire, and did what I could with it though I was already hot, for I liked how it glowed orange against the night. I sat back from it and enjoyed the flames, watching them dance in the night.

There were jackals in the distance, I listened to their cries; but I dozed then, nodding by the hot fire, until I felt a presence near me, and the smell of something foul. Instinctively I turned away from it, but then I jerked awake because it came to me through my sleep that there were jackals near me.

Their footsteps were soft and I watched their quivering tails, paralysed with fear, for their mouths were dripping with saliva and their golden eyes that flashed in the light of the fire had a hint of the madness that comes with hunger. But there was cunning too in those eyes and their ears were alert and their mouths hung open.

They circled the fire on tiptoe, their slender bodies moving in a deft manner, and I watched the foam drip from their jaws. One came nearer than the rest. His muzzle was soft and his nose was moist and he stood so close to me that I could have reached out and stroked him. He raised his head and sniffed this unfamiliar smell, his nose twitching above me. I closed my eyes and when I opened them I saw that his were staring into mine. I wasn't scared, but I felt vulnerable lying down. I pushed myself upwards so that I was leaning on one elbow, so slowly that he wouldn't notice. There were seven of them. I remained like that for some time, the jackals rummaging around the fire, unearthing scraps of food. There were three younger ones, close to their mother, and two older ones. It was the father who stood closest to me looking into my eyes.

My arm grew stiff beneath me, until they moved away to the lake, and drank there, encouraging the young ones to drink, and while I watched them I realised that I felt happy, more knowledgeable about things, what exactly I couldn't say, but a dart of ecstasy rushed through me, and I felt that I was better for what I had seen. I turned around and Saleem was there, sitting in the shade of his tent, and I read in his eyes what I was thinking.

You been there long? I said.

He said, were you scared, tell me, were you scared? When you were sleeping and he was right up against your face? That was the adult male.

You saw everything?

Everything. I was just coming out. I couldn't sleep and I heard something. I saw them approaching but it was too late to warn you.

I didn't know you were there.

He said, it was amazing wasn't it? They completely surrounded you. They acted like you weren't here, like you are nothing. He lit a cigarette. Were you shaking, he said, when he came right up to you?

I don't know, I said. I didn't have time to think about what I was thinking and now I can't remember.

He was striding towards me. The cigarette glowed in his hand. It was something, he said. I almost think they didn't realise you were human. They weren't scared of you. There were two helpers, he said. Did you notice the helpers?

Helpers?

It's unique to jackals, he said. Sometimes the grown offspring remain with their parents, assist the new family, they help guard the cubs and they also bring them food. He stared out into the darkness, where the cry of the jackals drifted back to us through the night. Their remaining on as helpers, he said, increases the family's chance of survival.

After that, any unease between us was gone. We sat awake all night drinking Turkish coffee, and he told me about his life; the fire grew pale and eventually went out, and the butt of his cigarette glowed orange in the night. Presently I told him about my life, the people who lived on the kibbutz, my mother, how she left and how she wrote me letters, though she hadn't at the beginning. It was as if she remembered me one day, I said. I told him about her children, how they lived in Holland and were much younger than me. But mostly we talked about his life, for it was fascinating to me – he had his own manner of thinking, his own definite ideas about the past.

When the sun ascended over the horizon, I was surprised because I had been planning to go to sleep. We sat back and allowed it to warm us, until it became too hot, and he said it was time for him to leave. He studied my foot before he left, his fingers probed my wound, examining it for shards of glass in the morning light.

*

The rain continues to fall on my skin and I look at the sky. Sometimes when winter is coming it is hard to imagine that night on the beach, the heat and the mosquitoes and the way summer felt to me then. David, I say, perhaps we should go inside. The lightning is flashing across the sky, and the rain that I waited for has come at last, the autumn rain, enormous, angry, incessant.

*

When I was fourteen years old my mother wrote to me to invite me to visit. You have a brother and a sister, she wrote, it is time you met them, Avi, indeed it is important that you meet them. It was June and summer beckoned, scorching summer days, filled with soccer, the beach and the sea, the cornfields, followed by warm nights, spent in whispers under the Eucalyptus trees that Father planted for my mother the summer I was born. You will come for a fortnight, she wrote, and we shall show you the Netherlands.

I stood there with the crisp white pages between my hands. Tell your father, she said, tell your father it is important that you see me, tell him that and he will bid you visit for a fortnight. Tell him it is necessary that you see me, for you do need to see me, my darling, even if you don't realise it. She beckoned to me, my mother, casting her magic from afar, bewitching me with her tales of long summer evenings in Holland, enchanting twilights, the taste of her home-made lemonade on summer days, the smell of crushed mint all around the kitchen, wandering to the promenade by the sea in the evenings, surrounded by the cultured atmosphere of Europe. I imagined standing in her sun-filled, polish-scented house that would enfold me in its depths so that I belonged there absolutely.

I mentioned it to my father on a June evening. It's important to her that I visit, I said, and struggled to find the words, it's important to me too, I said. He flinched and looked away, towards the mountains that he always wandered to when he needed to think; but then he turned towards me and there was something in his eyes that I dared not analyse – she told you to say that, he said, and he let forth a hard, mirthless laugh. You need to see her indeed.

He turned away from me then, we were in the garden outside his home, he began to pick at the weeds that grew amongst his geraniums. He tossed each weed onto the path, gathered them into untidy piles, dusted his hands, before plunging them deep into the soil, fingers searching for the roots, for they were deep in the earth. He moved then to the lilies, and began to remove the weeds that grew around Mother's lilies. Greedy feeders, he said, do you know how many plants suffer in return for these. They take all the goodness out of the earth. He waved his hand towards the great trumpet-shaped flowers that omitted an odour that spoke only of her.

Father, I said. He did not turn. I stood there for a time, behind him, but there were many weeds to be pulled from the ground and he did not turn, and the moon crept into the sky, it was bright, so that it seemed to be almost day. A perfect image of her came to me, sitting in her flat kingdom in Holland, I thought of her and the two children, I thought of them, my family, our family, and my soul yearned for her, my mother. Father, I said, Father, it is not important that I see these people. I have my family here, my friends are here, the kibbutz is my family. He did not turn, my father, he did not turn but his back relaxed, I saw the tension leave his shoulders. I walked away from him, kicked at a pile of weeds on the grass.

I did not write to her that summer, I did not write that June, nor July, even when August arrived I did not write. Until my first day at school. I wrote then, Mother, I said, Dear Mother, the summer was fun here and I decided not to visit. I hope you don't mind, maybe some other time. She didn't reply, not immediately, and when she did, it was a day much like this one, it was October and it was raining; never mind, she said, Avi, my son.

*

David, I say, David, let's go inside.

He doesn't move, keeps his head in his hands, and I see then that he is crying, and that there is a look of inexpressible sadness in his eyes. I never thought I'd be here now, he says, I never thought I'd be in a place like this. In years to come, what will I tell my children about what brought me here.

David, I say. I put my hand on his shoulder. Come in. He sits in the rain with his head in his hands, and finally when it is so hard it feels like it will pierce my skin, the wardens come and they are angry. What are you thinking, they shout, and I move inside, but David doesn't, he sits with his head in his hands, until eventually they run through the rain and drag him inside.

Chapter Eight

People have long memories, you said. When you looked back, you said, it seemed that much of your life was made up of other peoples' memories. Is it the same with your people, you asked, and I couldn't answer because for most of my life there was just me and Father.

You are walking home from school with Lafi, he is in the same class as you and because he lives on your street you always walk home together. Karim is behind you, kicking at a stone so that it bounces off your leg whenever he hits his target. You turn to him and raise your fists, but you keep walking with Lafi.

When you arrive at your house, you turn to leave Lafi, but you run after him then because there is something you remembered that you have to tell him, and the two of you stand for a time, laughing in the sunshine, until eventually you follow Karim down the driveway. Now you are kicking at stones, because you have homework to do, and the evening stretches long before you.

You walk into the kitchen, into the smell of baking bread, and Grandmother is there, and she is very stern. Come with me, she says when you arrive, reaching for you and Karim. You put your bag on the table but this was not the right thing to do. Not there, it's filthy, your bag, she hisses, and you shove it to the floor. Come, she says. What did I tell you? Follow me. The other children are inside already.

You notice that her lips are redder than usual and that she is wearing a nice dress, too nice a dress for working in the kitchen, baking bread.

I'm hungry, Karim says, but she frowns at him.

You can wait, she says. Your generation know nothing about hunger. She leads you through the kitchen, clutching each of you by the wrist, through the dark hall, before pausing outside a room that is always locked. Grandmother's room, you call it, for she often sits there in the evenings, you see her there from outside, her silhouette against the shutters. Once Karim climbed up the wall and peered in the window, but you never dared to look at this room.

Karim says, why are we going here? We never go here. I've never been here. He is backing away from her, from the room, and you pull back too. Children, she says, without opening her mouth. She is trying to be quiet. Children, you absolutely must behave or you will be severely punished this evening.

We never go to this room, Karim says. I don't want to go to this room.

Your father ordered us, she says. It is an important occasion and he wants us to use this room. He thinks we should use it more often. She releases her grip on Karim's wrist and raises her hand to knock. It is all he needs; she realises his intention to escape and grasps for his arm, but he senses freedom and runs, footsteps hard upon the marble floor and disappears into the kitchen. She curses under her breath and grasps your wrist tighter, you feel her hands bruising your skin. She raises her hand. She knocks.

Yes, says your father's voice. Come in.

In, she says to you. Get in. She opens the door and pushes you into the room in one movement, and you stand in front of Father, blinking, attempting to adjust your eyes to the bright light in the room. The door clicks closed behind you. You are confused; this room is just like the room in the Jewish lady's house, large with white walls, a huge oak table before the window. There are two patterned chairs and a matching couch facing them, a small coffee table with a glass panel in the centre placed between them, a bunch of lavender hanging on the wall – the room is full of its scent – and there is a bowl of fruit on the coffee table.

You stand in front of Father. He is seated in one of the patterned chairs, an identical chair to the one you saw in the Jewish lady's house, the same angle where she sat that day, the same streak of light cast across his face.

Father, you say.

The other boys are all crammed together on the patterned couch, where Grandmother sat that day in the house in Safsaf. Little Sulieman's face is filthy, though he is wearing his best clothes.

Karim is not well, Grandmother says. I sent him to his room.

Father nods. Sit Saleem, he says.

You move to the couch and the other boys wriggle to make room for you. You sit. And then you glance at the woman. She is seated beside Father in the other patterned chair, her chair placed slightly behind his. Her eyes meet yours and there is a smile in them. Your father turns to her. This is Basmah, he says. Basmah, this is my eldest son, Saleem.

She looks straight at you. She says, I've heard about you,

Saleem, you are a very big boy, bigger than I was expecting. You smile, and you wish Karim hadn't run away.

I'm the biggest in my class, you say. Grandmother sighs, but Basmah is nodding and smiling.

It is then you notice that the vase is on the oak table, your vase, from the Jewish lady's house, placed there in the same position as it was in the old house. You feel a leap of joy when you see it, a recognition, for you came to love it in the nights it rested between your hands as you slept, before your grandmother removed it from your bed.

Now boys, Father says, you will be getting to know Basmah in the next weeks. We are to marry next month. She will become like a mother to you all. You must be good boys, do you hear me?

You all nod in unison. You count the years in your head, the time that Mother has been dead. One. Two. Three. Four. Five. August, she died in August, you don't remember the date, and nobody mentions Mother now, so instead you think of her harder all August.

Basmah will see what good boys you are. You nod. And if Basmah needs anything, you will all help her.

Grandmother coughs. You will be very good children, she says. She is turning to leave, and nodding to dismiss you, but there is something you need to tell Father before you go.

This room, you say. Father, this room is the same room as the room in Safsaf.

Grandmother is frowning. Saleem, she says, boys only speak when they are spoken to.

But Father didn't see the room, you say. The room in Safsaf. It is just the same as this. Why are we sad about Safsaf when we have the same room here?

Grandmother places a hand on your shoulder and squeezes it hard. Her lips are white with fury. Not now, she says, not now.

Basmah turns to Father. What room? she says.

I have no idea, says Father. What room in Safsaf, Saleem? His face is stern, his eyes too.

The room where I got the vase, you say, and you point towards the table.

Silence, says your grandmother, there is no need for this now. Her hand is squeezing your shoulder, and you stare hard at the plaid pattern on the couch, each swirl ending in a green curl. You place your finger against the pattern and you know then that this was her secret, this room and its contents, reconstructed with love and sadness, and an attention to detail that only the weighty memory of what was lost can bring, designed to mirror the room she loved, the home she once had, silently guarded and maintained, seldom used, but always there.

Her voice is ice. It's nothing, she says. The child is confused, it must look like that other room to him. You can go now, boys, and you all rush to leave, each one of you trying to reach the door first. Karim is in your room when you get there.

What was that about? he says.

Father is getting married.

He begins to sob. His nose begins to run the way it always does when he cries. He lies on his bed and he cries. Grandmother is in the kitchen and you hear the sound of pots being moved around, and later Father goes to your room and slaps Karim for running away from Grandmother; and you move outside to the yard where you can't hear Karim crying, and kick your football against the wall. The ball thuds against the wall and back to you, and you know Father will come, and when he does you feel his presence behind you but you don't turn.

Saleem, he says. Do not mention Safsaf like that again. It is not your right to remind Grandmother of the past and the things that happened to her, the things she lost.

Sorry, you say.

It is not the same room anyway, he says. It can't be.

It is, you whisper, and you kick your ball hard against the wall, but that makes him angry.

Saleem, he says, your grandmother says it is not the same room. There are certain similarities all right, but it is not the same as the room in Safsaf.

You hold the football in your hands but still you don't turn to him. You stand facing the wall, you can smell urine where the feral cats mark their territory every night. Father, you say, you didn't see the room. You were not in it. Grandmother said you only lived in it when you were very small.

He hits you across the back of the head, and your face smashes against the wall, cracking open your forehead, and blood trickles down your face. Father, you gasp, and you swallow your own blood. He says, it is not your right to speak of these things. You don't understand about the past, you are not old enough to understand it, we don't expect you to understand. But do not speak of what you do not understand.

There is blood in your mouth, mingling with the salt of the tears, and you strain with all your body to keep those tears from overflowing. Sorry, Father, you say.

You will apologise to your grandmother.

Yes, you say.

Follow me, he says. He leads you to the kitchen. She is standing erect over a pot of soup, stirring it over the heat, her mouth set firmly; her face is wet, and you don't know if it is because she is hot or because she has been crying. Sorry, Grandmother, you say. She doesn't turn to you, instead she nods once, an affirmation that she accepts the apology.

Tell her you know it is not the same room, your father says.

I know it is not the same room, you say. After that you don't go back to the room, nor do you speak about it to anybody.

Did you come to understand about the past, the importance of it to them, I asked, but no, you said, there is nothing to be found there, that's all you learnt about the past. Bricks are bricks, you said, and anyone who spends their time grieving for bricks, for a room that stares out over white mountains, for a vase on an oak table, their life stands still, you said. There is nothing for them.

Chapter Nine

July 30th, 1990

Dear Sareet,

Thank you for your letter. I received it on the anniversary of your departure from this kibbutz, and indeed from this country. It is hot, yes, July is a painful month here. The kibbutz is very much as I am sure you remember it, today was most similar to the day you left, there has been no release from this heat for almost two weeks, though now that it is evening the hot haze of the day has lifted somewhat, and there is a very slight breeze. The same plants that I watered this morning are wilting after the heat of the day. How optimistic I was this morning after I irrigated them, thinking foolishly it was enough water for at least two days! Do you ever think of the July day that you left all of this behind you, the people who once filled your life, the heat of that summer – it almost destroyed you, you said.

For some reason I imagine you reading this letter in a very European room: high-ceilinged with enormous windows, a book-lined wall, an empty fireplace, sitting alone at an ebony black desk, a manicured garden beyond the bay window, an exact square of lawn surrounded by a strip of concrete, your children playing quietly in a sandpit. They have manners, these children, they are quiet and civilised, they do not make unreasonable demands, cry and shout and scream, scratch, lash out, throw tantrums in supermarkets. Beyond you are more houses, similar to that of your own, semi-detached pretty houses, suburbia. Somewhere inside you there was always the longing for suburbia, perhaps you finally discovered a place where you belong absolutely. Beyond you are the flat plains of Amsterdam, unadorned with hill or tree, dazzling brightly in the sunshine, a gentle sun, kind and benevolent and not too hot, the window is open and the fresh air drifts in to you, vaguely perfumed by the tidy row of roses you grow at the back of the garden.

I am writing to you as though the years since we last met have fallen away, as though we were standing face to face, here on our patio with the scent of your lilies (I've never liked them though continue to grow them, yet I admit their brief summer display is quite magnificent, though short-lived) all around us.

To answer your question, I am not sure, in fact I have no idea, as to why Avi has not written to you for two months. I have received no indication from him that this is the case, nor do I have any idea as to his motives in not writing, if indeed there are any. Surely you realise that we do not speak of you often, or does your own shameless vanity allow you to believe that we do? You must remember that he has not seen you for exactly nine years, a lifetime for a fourteen-year-old boy.

You left him, and all that was his, everything he knew; you live another life in another country with other children whom he has never seen. He has not learnt from me who his mother is, from me he learns nothing of you. It is far more likely that when you left some favourite images of you remained with him, linking him to you, living within him, so that his image of you has not aged, for Avi you are just the same as you were that July. Nothing is different.

My own belief is that it is probable he has not written because he is enjoying his summer holidays, and the routine of the winter months is nonexistent for him.

You ask me to describe to you how he spends his days? Given that it is difficult to pinpoint what exact details you want, I will describe a typical day in his summer for you. Avi wakes early, far earlier than most of his peers, it has always been that way with him, and sometimes he visits me in the gardens while he waits for his friends to appear. It's cool in the gardens in the early mornings, in fact it is the time when most of the work gets done, for the sun seems to be extraordinarily hot this year, and he helps me with my work. Most of his ideas are quite impractical; he loves to read my gardening books and he often wants to plant flowers that are native to the British Isles here on the kibbutz, a semi-arid region! Of course, I explain to him that it is impossible to grow such plants under these conditions, the sun is cruel I tell him, they cannot possibly thrive in this climate, but he believes with special care it is very possible. We argue about it and at times I have given in to him, with the understanding that once planted, these non-native plants will be his responsibility. But then there are mornings that he sleeps late, or his friends rise early, or he simply forgets, and they wilt and die. He despairs when he finds them like this, tries to revive them with copious amounts of water, but it is pointless growing non-native plants in this sun, which is why I do not assist him in his endeavours. I refuse to irrigate the non-native plants when he neglects his duties. There are things he needs to learn.

His friends appear in time for breakfast, and after they eat there are a number of things they like to do. One of their favourite pastimes is soccer; they play it most mornings, continuing from the relative cool of the morning directly after breakfast until midmorning when the sun becomes a golden furnace in the sky. Avi is a master at soccer, the moment his feet touch the ball he becomes a kind of king among the other children; how can I describe him to you? He always plays barefoot, he is fast and nimble, he dodges through the older boys, his supple brown body weaving in and out between them. He is a consistent footballer, a good team player, an asset to a team, unafraid to take risks. They can play soccer like this, even in this sun, for one hour, two hours, pausing occasionally for water. Avi hurls it over his head so that his hair sticks to his forehead, and the water trickles down his face, mingling with the sweat.

Soccer is their morning pastime, they never tire of it, but the sun is hot and eventually one of the boys, hair soaked with sweat, will suggest another activity, perhaps a trip to the fields, where there is the shelter of the plants and sometimes the cool water of the irrigation system. Then, off they race, through the dirt that clings to their sandals, their feet, their ankles, accumulates under their nails, inside their nostrils, to the kibbutz fields, where the corn, tomatoes and watermelons are growing. They particularly love to play in the cornfields, the ears of corn tower over their heads, and of course if Moshe Levi (do you remember him?) catches them he becomes very angry, and his red face turns purple, though he rarely does catch them. Do you remember how the corn reaches up towards the sky at this time of year? You used to love to walk amongst it in the evenings, the sound of the sprinklers, that cool splash of water on your face in the dust of a summer evening in Galilee.

They eat lunch together in the dining room, I encourage Avi to take a siesta, but he tries to avoid this, along with his peers, and in the afternoon they make their way to the beach, where they plunge into the water, only their soaked heads visible among the waves, their voices carried towards the shore by the sea breeze. When they have had their fill of the salt water they lie on the sand, and presently they begin to play soccer again, this time on the beach, until they become too hot and run again to the waves, where they remain until nightfall.

Clumps of the rough sand from the beaches in this region are permanently pasted to his skull, and he smells of the sea and the dust of summer. He is of average height for his age, with burnished white-gold hair that reaches to his shoulders, golden sun-scorched skin, a firm athletic body – he is not the child that you remember. How could he be, Sareet?

Though I admit that I do wonder sometimes as I watch them among the waves, I wonder if Avi feels that he is different to them. Does he seem to them to be a boy with no past, for let's face it, unlike them there are no siblings, no rooms filled with family portraits, no relatives who come and visit during the holidays. There is a sadness about him, a knowingness, that is impossible to describe. I see it in him sometimes, on rare occasions admittedly, but it is there nonetheless, and I've noticed that he stands back from things, does not thrust himself forward into everything, as his peers do. There is a shyness about him, a reluctance to be in the spotlight, and when I see it in him it wrenches at my heart, and I wonder was he always that boy or did he become that boy when you left.

In the evening when he returns home he eats a light meal (we no longer eat our evening meal in the kibbutz dining room, apart from Fridays and holiday eves), and then disappears with his friends again. Their night activities are more furtive, less open, though I usually take a walk around the kibbutz at this time, and I spot them sitting around under the Eucalyptus trees that grow behind the laundry, their whispers a part of the night here, familiar as the screaming jackals, and the sudden silences that echo through these mountains. They sit in the same spot as that in which their predecessors once sat, grown men and women now; it is the same now as it was then, nothing has changed.

Soon he will return to school – the summer is short – routine will return to his life in the autumn, and I believe he will write to you again then, he has not forgotten, nor will he forget. In answer to your question, yes, I remember when he came home that time, when he was very ill with scarlet fever and they sent him home to be with us. I have not forgotten those nights, you lying beside him watching as he slept, huddled up, his cheeks burning red, his breath heavy, his hair barely visible over the blanket that was bunched against his forehead – how could I forget? They are only memories now, Sareet, our combined memories, he is nothing of that child now.

How still this July night is. I can almost touch the silence. Tranquillity has descended on the kibbutz, and the heat and sweat of tomorrow is almost impossible to imagine. Now a slight breeze is moving through the Cyprus trees, now a cat is climbing the little lemon tree that you planted here the summer you left, now an army patrol is moving along the distant border, lights beaming across the surrounding hills, the tangled barbed wire a black mass behind them, the beams of light reassuring in the black darkness. Beyond my garden a television set flickers in a neighbour's house, and beyond that house two lovers are sitting drinking wine on their patio – she is whispering in his ear and he is leaning towards her. It is time for bed.
Daniel

Chapter Ten

I've packed, she says. I'm ready. Even if we had to go suddenly I am ready.

She is dizzy with her plans. I look at my hands, dirty from working in the gardens, like Father's always were when I was a boy and he held me as I tried to sleep, his calloused hands against my bare skin in the heat of the summer.

I've been very clever, she says. I'm sure no one has noticed. Even Karim. She leans against the gauze.

There are no loud visitors around us today. Instead there is just muttered whispering, the air is full of acceptance and resignation, the distant sound of a woman sobbing, and Sahar's voice seems loud in the silence. I told my mother, she says.

I raise my eyes to her. Stupid girl.

It's okay, she says. I trust her. She understands everything.

Nobody understands everything.

She looks away from me. I had to, she says. I had to tell her. I want her to take care of my canary. And some other things too. I don't want Karim to take him.

What did she say?

She understands. She won't tell anyone.

She must have said something.

She just hopes you will be good to me. She looks up at the clock. I will come next week, she says. There will be last minute things you need to say to me. You may need me to do something for you? She glances around, at the other visitors. I won't miss this place, she says.

Silence.

Avi, she says. Avi, you aren't saying anything. Avi, what is it? Her fingers clasp her wrist and it becomes white under the grip.

I think of the beach. It's not going to work, I say. I finger the leather strap of my watch, Father's watch. I can't. I'm sorry. I've tried.

Avi, she says. It has to work. We have to do this. There are no other options.

There are always options.

She jerks back in her chair and stands, glances around her, at the people sitting and muttering in the surrounding cubicles. A moth is fumbling around the bare light bulb over her head, she turns to me. You know I have no other options.

Please go now, I say, but she laughs, a harsh laugh, and the couple in the next cubicle stare through the wire. I'm not going.

Well, soon you will have to leave, I say.

Why, she says. She looks straight at me. What is this about? Is it about Saleem?

She stands before me. A woman, not much more than a girl, dark hair, eyes that know things about the world, a mole on her forehead, over her right eye, lips that look better without lip gloss, small hands that I picture against my skin; she leans forward, these hands outstretched, pressed against the gauze.

It's the only thing I will ever ask you, she says. I promise. Never again will I ask anything of you. Please.

She has no hopes or expectations, no dreams of a detached house by the sea, a large garden with a south-facing patio to sit out on in the summertime. Such dreams are beyond her, standing as she does in a dark prison in a hot place, a place she does not like. She stands as she is, in complete possession of this November afternoon, as if it belongs to her, this place, me, and everything in it. She stands in front of me with dust upon her face, and when she rubs her eyes, she leaves a black streak of mascara across her cheek, the way she always does when she wears makeup, so that I feel a smile inside me for a moment. She doesn't expect absolute happiness, doesn't believe in it and I like her for that, like that she takes what she can from life and runs with it, clasping it to her. I like how she moves so softly within her world, how everything about her reflects him so exactly; and I want her to talk to me, tell me her plans, because when she does I listen to her voice and it feels safe, like when I was a young boy and my mother lay beside me as I was falling asleep, that feeling just when sleep was coming and I was safe and she was there.

Her fingers scratch at her cheeks. She turns her face toward me. Avi, I'll make you happy. I'll do anything you ask. Anything.

Zaki coughs behind me. We need a few more minutes, Zaki.

That's not your right.

I know it's not my right. I'm just asking a question, okay. He is reaching for his keys that hang on the belt around his waist.

Avi, she hisses at me, for I have antagonised him.

Have yourself a smoke, I say. I reach into my pocket and take out a packet of Gitanes. Have one, I say. They are good cigarettes. Father used to smoke one every evening. We are not allowed to smoke them here. No foreign cigarettes.

I know the rules, he knows the rules, he takes one, and as he takes it he looks me squarely in the eyes. He points the cigarette at me. Five minutes, he says. Five minutes and then it's goodbye. Goodbye. He makes a kissing sound with his lips and she recoils.

She is silent. She doesn't plead with me anymore, doesn't look at me; she stares at the ground, the dust that has piled up, from people walking in and out, bringing the smell of autumn to this sterile place, for dust has a scent, I realise then. She moves her toes around in the dust making swirling shapes on the floor. She raises her eyes. I watch Zaki smoking and she watches him too until he is exactly halfway through it, then she turns back to me, but still she doesn't speak.

We regard each other, and there is a light of recognition in her eyes, something like the last gleam of a match before the flame is snuffed out. For a moment she recognises me completely, knows me, and a part of me that I don't want to recognise reaches out to that part; but then life goes out of her visibly, absolutely, so that she lets out a gasp, a deep breath, swallowed far into her lungs, and expels it in one go. She turns and walks away – I don't call after her and she doesn't look back.

I stand up, I want to call after her, but the words don't come; I have to tell her something, a promise, an amount of how much I can give, I try to estimate that, but my mind is empty. I want to tell her about the dead, how they come back, how they always come back. I look at Zaki's cigarette, it's burnt down now, but he hasn't stubbed it out, it's between his fingers and his hand is halfway to his open mouth. He is watching the doorway. I watch the doorway too, long after she has vanished, so that the shadow it throws across the floor grows longer, the whispered conversations around me become less urgent, tired. I smoke too, and Zaki takes another one, and then eventually he begins to bring the other prisoners back to their cells, leaving me to watch the empty doorway.

*

My mother sent me a present for my tenth birthday. It is an important birthday, she wrote, you are now a decade old. I read the card first, it arrived three days before my birthday. I didn't open the present until the morning of my birthday. Father granted me permission to open it but I couldn't bring myself to tear open the paper she had touched. I imagined her wrapping it, her tongue against her lip as she concentrated on folding the paper around the present, the cool scent of her perfume, the sound of her other children squabbling in the background.

I opened it carefully, peeling away the layers of paper, my nails scraping against the tape, until eventually an oval snow globe fell out into my hands. There was a girl inside, a blonde girl with pink Wellington boots and anxious eyes, clutching the hand of a fat toddler in a red woolly hat and green coat. I stood with it in my hands, and Father stood behind me, and we both looked at it for a time, until eventually he found the words.

Shake it, he said, give it a shake.

I shook it and the snow began to fall around them, so that the two figures seemed to stand closer together. I watched them for a long time, shaking the globe sometimes, and then the snow would fall again. They stood in front of an old stone house that looked like a castle. My mother had two other children then, a boy and a girl, and it seemed to me on that day, my tenth birthday, that those were the children in the snow globe. When I imagined them and their life in Holland, it was those children I saw, it was that stone house they lived in; and they played in the snow, threw snowballs at each other, wrapped themselves in the immensity of that coldness, before returning to the warm house, the fireplace, warm toast with melted butter, thick vegetable soup, while I swam in the warm sea.

Sometimes I would take the snow globe, shake it hard and watch the snow falling on the frozen figures inside and stare at them, standing as they did in their frozen wintry world where summer never came, even when the white summer sky of my country burnt beyond them. I came to believe absolutely that they were indeed my mother's children, her northern children, different from this barefooted, long-haired Middle Eastern child. I knew their kind, I had seen plenty of European movies. I knew how they dressed, knew they were well mannered, that they said excuse me and thank you, that they had Santa Claus and Christmas cake and holidays that seemed more fun than my own.

I always felt cold when I watched them. I always shivered, the coldness starting in my shoulders and running down my spine until I was cold all over. Even in the summer. And at school, when my teacher read about such places, those northern European countries with their secretive forests, endless grey skies, frozen winters, and roaring rivers, I listened with all my heart to her voice, for it spoke to me of my mother, her family, and their life there. I never stopped loving her, so that her touch remains upon my skin even today, even here.

*

Zaki comes back, pulls a chair close to mine and lights another cigarette. There is ash on his moustache.

You ready to go back, he says.

Yes, I say. I am ready.

He leads me to my cell but he is different, moves quietly, and when I enter my cell he doesn't slam the metal door behind me.

Do you need anything? he asks.

No, nothing.

The small window is open so that I hear the rain outside. It's not heavy, just a dull sound, a constant presence, and I feel cold then, I hate the sound of rain. I lie on my bed for a time until all the light goes out of the day and I begin to write. I'm desperate now, I need to finish this before I leave, so that these stories and people remain here in the desert, perhaps where they belong, among the stones, and rocks, and cracks, to rest here, so that they reside somewhere at least; and maybe with time they will become less sharp, less glaring, kinder and more forgiving.

Chapter Eleven

November 14th, 1990

Dear Sareet,

I received your letter two weeks ago, and apologise for the delay in replying for you gave me much to think about. I've walked a lot, and I've given it some thought, as you requested.

For the first week after receipt of your letter I allowed myself to believe that you could come back, and I nestled in that dream for eight days. In fact for the duration of these eight days I existed in a kind of stupor: I went to bed early, slept well and my dreams were pleasant, and in turn my days were spent in a happy haze of planning what to do with the house in preparation for your return. On the eighth day I decided I must write to you immediately and tell you that, yes, indeed, it is a good idea that you come back, as you say you want to. I made the decision early one morning, after a sleepless night, my first sleepless night for eight days, surrounded by the winter sound of rain. You know all about rain, you say, but you chose that rain, and everything else about your life now.

I was tired, it had been a stormy night, and I had

woken from a strange dream where I strolled through a dark forest filled with little natural light, heavy with the scent of damp leaves, that opened on to a great lake under the grey British skies of my childhood – the leaves thick under my feet, the mouldy smell of autumn all around me. It beckoned to me all night, this autumnal forest, remaining with me after I awakened; but something else, what I am not sure, it murmured something to me, what exactly I cannot remember. I think it was my mother's silhouette I saw there, standing by the lake; she was shivering and she called out something to me, but her words disappeared into the cold air. The night was long and I arose before dawn and sat at the window, drinking sweet coffee and staring at the rain, great sheets of it, driving against the house. When it eased I decided that I must take my morning walk.

So, having decided I must write to you to tell you to hasten your journey back, I walked through the rain, out of the kibbutz, towards the chalk mountains in the distance, silver and shimmering in the wet morning light. I'll write this morning, I thought, and after that I must tell Avi immediately, best to get it done with: Mother wants to come home, and I've agreed that she should.

I imagined you here, here this very winter, making it your home again, repossessing us, me, Avi, our very house where even the colours of the walls remain the same as they were when you were here. Avi doesn't sleep in the house, of course, you remember that – he sleeps with the other children, as is the way here, or had you forgotten? Nor would your other children, the girl and boy, children I don't know, whose very names elude me, sleep with us in the house. You realise that, don't you? Are you sure you want to bring them here, to a world they do not know, a world that would be strange to them, leaving their father behind, as you once left us?

I sat there on the mountain, a place I've visited often over the years, both in winter and summer. The rain stopped and it was quiet there, save for the sound of water, surging down the mountainside, and I looked down on the kibbutz. The gardens are different from that distance, from above, and I see things there that I would not notice on my normal rounds. That morning, for instance, I realised that the wisteria I have been cultivating all these years does not belong on the western wall of the children's house. I won't go into the details, but once observed I knew that it was absolutely wrong there and would have to be moved, though moving wisteria is a troublesome business – you know how difficult it is about flowering. In fact I knew at that moment that I only planted it there when Avi was a boy so that the scent would come to him as he slept.

After that observation I did what I don't normally do, I lit a cigarette. Generally speaking, I save this cigarette for the evening, one cigarette a day, that's all I allow myself; but that morning I broke my strict rules and I smoked one, for I came to a realisation there on the rain-soaked mountainside. I remembered something and that remembrance, that stab of memory, made me realise that you absolutely must not come back. You see, the exact detail of the day you left came to me, I hadn't thought of it in a long time; I once thought of it often, once I saw the image of you leaving a thousand times in a single afternoon, for years and years. When I stopped seeing it I can't remember, but I thought of it that morning and I remembered your eyes, the life inside them dying, how dull they became; and I wondered how life with us died for you as completely and utterly as it did. I remembered you stirring your coffee that morning, the tears running down your face, because of the constant heat you said.

It's different now, of course – we have air conditioning and life is comfortable. The management committee has become more lenient about privately owned luxuries, too lenient I often think, and I am not the only member of this community who feels like this. There are more than enough comforts, I am sure you would you enjoy them. I tried to convince myself of that.

But mostly I remembered what you said. It hit me with a blow to the chest that morning on the mountainside, even all these years later, your words of that July day still contain the same powers of destruction that they did then. Do you remember? You said that youth is above all a collection of possibilities, and that with every day you spent with me another of those opportunities died. Died before your eyes, you said. Do you know how it feels to watch those opportunities die, you said. I can't stay here and watch them die anymore, you said.

That summer is still inside me – the daze through which I laboured in the gardens, the greenfly that devoured the rose garden, only detected when it was far too late for action, the weeds that overcame the display of colour opposite the communal laundry, the rows of putrid strawberries that I neglected to harvest, the buzzing of the swollen flies around them – is still with me. You have not forgotten it either, that summer is still inside you, it returns to you every year. To return here would be a kind of release for you.

After you left I felt nothing for a long time, I continued as normal because I had to, and Avi needed me too. I am not sure, for example, for how long I set the table, on a Saturday evening (when the dining room was closed in deference to the Sabbath) for three people, something I had done automatically for so long. I only know that I did it for a long time, and neither of us looked at or acknowledged the extra plate, yet it was always there, and I continued to do it after I remembered that you were gone. After a time it ceased to be an automatic gesture, but I did it just the same, because I realised that the Saturday that I stopped setting a place for you would be the day that I understood and accepted that you weren't coming back, and I sensed that Avi needed me to leave that place for you.

That place is gone, Sareet: the plate, the knife, the fork, all the memories and hopeless love that went with the setting of a place for you. We both believed for years, you see, that you would come back. There were no words for what we believed, but nevertheless we believed it absolutely. Words are not always necessary, and now, long after we stopped believing, you say you want to come back. You left us, but that summer never did, it clung to us for years, lived inside us, the heat and the dust and the hopelessness of everything. And your tears. And your leaving. It still clings to us today.

You must realise that this is not an easy decision for me to make, but I believe it to be the right one.

I would rather you not mention the nature of your request to the boy. The fact is that you left him once, and when you did his welfare became my responsibility. I simply believe it is better for him to understand that people do leave and don't come back. I am not sure that he would benefit from you bursting back into his life, you and all the endless drama that is part of life with you, an integral part of life with you. It would also be easier for me if you continued as before, and wrote only to the boy. It's preferable to forget all about this business now. I am sorry if this is stark, it is not as I meant it, but I know it to be the right decision, that you have merely lost interest in your Dutch adventure, for some reason you have lost the heart for it all.

And because I know it wouldn't work. There is little left for you and I, Sareet, little is left of that time and the people we were then, nothing is left of your youth and my energy. You now believe that you would be content to simply come home to us, to this small community, live here again, live this uncomplicated life style after the life you have lived in Amsterdam. You speak of the smell of Avi's skin after you bathed him, the odour of cheeses and olives and coffee that greeted you at the door of the communal dining room each morning, the storms that blaze across Galilee in the winter, the streaks of lightning across the sky, gleaming against the horizon. What happened to you that you discarded your life here, the people that filled it, suddenly and ruthlessly and with the blind persistence that I came to expect of you? Or does it matter? For the loss is there, whether or not you realise what it is you lost, or when, or why, and the reason no longer matters.

An empty autumn evening is falling on the Galilee, and I have said all there is to say. It is late, the rain is battering the windows, the thunder rolls in the distance. I am reminded of the young soldier I was when I met you and the summer that followed, that first summer after the war. Do you remember when we first met on the steps outside the kibbutz dining room, came face to face for the first time. How you reached out and squeezed my wrist to welcome me home that day, as many people did, but there was only you! Do you remember that first summer, sitting outside on those airless evenings, your head on my shoulder, gazing up through the branches at the stars in the summer sky? The smell of the Sinai desert was still upon me then, the faces of my comrades and enemies return to me in my dreams; that time has never really gone away, and, perhaps for this reason, neither have you.

None of this matters anymore, I shall go to sleep.

Daniel

Chapter Twelve

It must have been dawn on the beach. I remember a vague light on the horizon, the smell of coffee, the taste of cigarettes, and a coldness – for the fire had gone down and the dawn air was cool. I remember your face as you weaved your story, your voice as it stumbled over these events.

There was no sense of victory that day, you said. There was nothing.

You are eighteen now, a man, the second man of the family after Father. The letter has arrived, your grandmother has placed it unopened on your bed. You stare at it for a long time, you sit on your bed and you stare at it, for you recognise the words stamped across the front of it, you know what is inside without opening it: inside will be a date, a time, there will be words, an appointment, exactly as you expected. You note the objects in your room: Karim's bed, your own bed, your clothes folded on the shelves, your books, arranged in alphabetical order, the picture of the veiled woman that has always hung in this room.

You open it in one swift movement, you note the date, the time, and afterwards you move towards this date, making the appropriate arrangements, packing your most suitable clothing. Three days before you are due to go you tell Grandmother.

I am beginning my army service in three days, you say.

She is scrubbing pots, she doesn't turn. You wait, you

stand there, her back is stiff and you know she will speak. You watch her shadow on the wall, the sharp beak-like nose, she speaks without turning.

Where are you going, she asks.

I don't know, you say. They didn't say, I have to report to a base but after that I will be moved. I don't even know what I will be doing. She continues to scrub the pots. I will receive training for whatever I am doing, you say. That is standard.

Packing bags, she said, preparing someone else's parachute, placing it in a pack for them. Cooking their food, cleaning their toilets, that's what you'll be doing. They won't give someone like you any responsibility. She lifts a pot into the sink, grimaces at its weight, and begins to scrub.

Grandmother, you say, you don't know what you are talking about.

I know what I'm talking about, she says. I know what they think about our people. They will never give you any responsibility, never trust you, why would they? You are wasting your time and your youth. On them. You know nothing, every time you speak you reveal your ignorance.

I won't be back for a while, you say. It will be a few weeks, maybe months. I will phone.

She scrubs the pot, bent double over the sink, her once dark hair has gone grey, you note that now and you wonder that you didn't notice it happening, you didn't see the streaks of grey, the gradual lightening. Don't phone here, she says, we don't want tales of your heroics.

You turn to leave the kitchen, she stays where she is, bent

over the sink, a weak streak of light across her face, shining through the herbs she has growing on the windowsill of her kitchen: basil, parsley and, always, rosemary. You pack your clothes, alone, you've never packed for such a long period of time, you are sure you will forget something. The days pass, hot days, cloudless skies, and all the time you wait, nobody speaks to you about your army service, nobody asks you where you are going, or when you will be back, and the bright hot days are endless for the waiting.

The day comes, and when you awake, early, you close your eyes, and you will the sleep to come for another moment. You think of your mother, you remember her touch, the light way she moved, her bare feet on the cold floor, you remember how she used to say the past is exactly that – the past; you remember this house, how it was when it was still filled with her. Karim is sleeping in his bed. Bye, Karim, you say, but he does not open his eyes. You watch him sleeping, but he is not sleeping, he is awake, and you turn from him. You open the window of your room, the heat pours in, you peer outside, at the women working in the fields picking swollen watermelons. They are like ants in the distance, and beyond them the mountains, and beyond these mountains, Safsaf. The smell of the jasmine drifts up from the yard and you gaze down at that dark place, sheltered by the walls of the surrounding houses. It is at the entrance to a small laneway opposite your window that the jasmine grows, clinging to life by draping itself around a weeping willow, planted by grandmother, opposite her kitchen window, a weeping willow tree, a safsaf, in memory of her other home, enabling it to spiral upwards towards the sun. You gaze at the blackened crates piled up in the corner, the rubbish strewn around – old shoes, even the bonnet of Uncle Sabri's blue minivan, rusted now, with holes in it – but still there is just the smell of jasmine.

You walk down the stairs and place your bags at the door. Grandmother is at the sink, and your father is sitting at the table, drinking his morning coffee. He nods at you, but your grandmother does not turn.

Do you want coffee? your father asks. No, you answer, no, I will get some on the way. He nods. Well, he says, off you go then. Goodbye, you say. I'll be back soon. He nods and stares into his coffee.

Goodbye Grandmother, you say, but she doesn't turn. She is slicing bread, fresh bread that she baked that morning.

It's best to go now, your father says, and you turn from them, and then Basmah is in the doorway, her eyes are smiling at you, and that catches your heart. I'm going, you say, and she follows you outside. Your bag, it's heavy, she says, your father will bring you to the bus station. No, you say, no, I'm okay, I will carry it myself. You'll phone, won't you, she says. Yes, you say, when I get a chance I will call.

You turn away from the house, the bus station is a blur in the distance, and you stumble over the cracks in the concrete. It's nothing, you tell yourself, three years, one of the elements of living in this country, becoming part of things, something we should have done long ago. You walk past two women drying watermelon seeds on a blanket, they nod at you and you smile in return. The morning sun is already hot on your back, and the house, Safsaf, your mother's grave, all of it is behind you, and the future is blank, you can colour it whatever colour you want, shape it to the shape of your thoughts, it is all your decision, all of it.

Chapter Thirteen

The rain is heavier now, the darkness is full of it, cracks of thunder explode across the night, each one returns to us again and again, through the darkness, the empty desert caves giving back to the night an answering cry. The jackals are silent, their thirst temporarily satiated by the rain, the hardship of summer has dissipated, and winter is yet to come. I cannot write, the onslaught of the late autumn rain has obliterated any desire to write, a deep exhaustion has descended upon me, the memories are suddenly vague, scattered, yet I cannot sleep, a sudden cold penetrates my bones. I hear David pacing up and down in his cell. Already the world is colder with the dust of summer gone from the air. I stand at my window and place my hands on the cool bars, lean my forehead against it but outside there is only darkness, and the rain.

Back at my desk now, the plastic is cold in my hands. I stare through the darkness at my photograph, captured before the explosion, the words on the page declaring that Avi Goldberg is a citizen of the United Kingdom. I trace my finger across the page. The pages are crisp and new, though there are traces of clay across them. The passport arrived at noon. We collect our post at the same time every day, after we have completed the morning work, before lunch is served, we stand in line and they call out our identification number. It was the first letter I received here, and for a fleeting moment

I thought it might be a letter from my mother, that her words might reach me here; only when I held the crisp envelope in my hands and read the typed words I realised that it could not possibly be from her, for how can she know that I am here. Yet for a brief moment, as I stepped forward to receive the letter, the anticipation of the boy was there again, the anticipation of walking home from school knowing there might be a letter from her, my mother; I reached out my hands and the guard passed it to me, a Russian guard, the monotony of his army service etched across his face. Our eyes met, there was contempt in his, I am unsure as to what he read in mine, and then the letter was in my hands, a padded envelope, a passport.

David paces about his cell, I hear him opening his window as far as he can until it crashes against the black bars. Gusts of cold air dart through my cell, for my window is already open and the wind rushes through in a great draft, I can taste the rain in it.

*

When I was four years old, my mother ran away. A May evening, she was standing on the patio uncorking a bottle of red wine, the sun was low, throwing fingers of orange across the sky. Father had returned home from the gardens, shirtless, his face red from the sun and glazed with sweat, he wore a purple handkerchief around his head. Let's drink some wine, she said, I'll just wash, he said, oh, come on, Daniel, she said, can't you just have a glass of wine as you are, you can shower afterwards. He hesitated, no, he said, I'd like to have a shower now.

I was sitting in the corner of the patio, playing with a fleet of John Deere tractors that I had accumulated over the years. A neat pile of soil lay in front of the parked tractors, waiting to be scooped up. My mother, her face flushed, placed the bottle of wine on the table and went indoors. After a time Father appeared on the patio, where is your mother, he said, where has she gone. He disappeared back indoors to search for her and when he reappeared he was muttering to himself. The bottle of wine was on the table, he poured himself a glass – she should be back soon he said aloud, wherever it is she has disappeared to.

Father sat back and sipped his wine, closed his eyes for a time. When the first traces of darkness appeared in the sky he sprung up, paced from one end of the patio to the other, stared into the distance – where is your mother, he said aloud, where can she be, and then something else, inaudible, under his breath. Gone, I said, and I crumbled balls of clay between my fingers. Father came towards me, grabbed my hands and dusted the soil from them.

I must look for her, he said, he picked me up and began to circle the kibbutz, where can she be, he murmured, what is wrong, where can she be. I must have grown heavy in his arms, for he placed me beside him and began to pull me after him. My legs grew tired and after a time he looked at me absently, I'll have to bring you to the children's house for the night, he said. He checked his watch, it's still early, he said. Never mind, someone will be there, and he strode towards the children's house, though I had begun to cry, for Mother was gone and my legs were weary, and we did not know where she was in the descending darkness.

Father, I said, I'll help find Mother, but he ignored my

pleas, and strode through the darkness towards the light of the children's house. Yefat was there, warm and soft, and anxious, she gathered my face to her chest; the poor boy, she said, it's early, he does not have to be back for almost another hour. Father explained to her that he had to leave me there, so she held me tight, and he strode away into the darkness to find my vanished mother.

I slept that night in the end, though I vowed to myself I would not sleep until my mother was safe; it came to me, descended upon me, an anxious tortured sleep, even now I remember that. I remember that night, waking in the darkness, raising my head to look around me, the peaceful breath of my sleeping comrades, the dim light where Yefat sat reading a book and humming to herself, the large windows of light the moon cast across the floor. And all the time knowing that she was gone, lost, that Father and I could not find her, could not locate her in the darkness.

*

Avi, David says, his whisper loud in the night, you are awake, I can hear you. He is pacing around his cell again, his footfall relentless, purposeful in the silence. Avi, he says, don't you wonder why I am here. You want to know why I'm here, don't you, Avi? You want to know?

David, I answer, we are all here by choice. I walk to the door of my cell, his face appears through the bars of the door opposite me. It's good to talk Avi, he says. A jackal howls in the distance, and I move to my window, waiting for dawn to arrive. One month, I say, I'm here for one month, you're here for one month. The time we should be in the Reserves doing our service. After that we leave, I say, that's it.

David calls after me, my last army service, he says. I sit down on the stone floor of my cell, trace my finger through the dust, the scar on my face throbs in the cooler night air. We were on the way to the territories, he says, when we were diverted. Some sort of protest, he says, things got out of control, and we were diverted there to help regain control of the situation. He sighs. A man, he says, a man got shot. I was near him.

I hear him shuffling around in the darkness, turning away from the door of his cell, moving back to the bars. I didn't pull the trigger, he says, but I was near him. I saw everything. He is silent for a few moments. He went down right away, he says. There was a woman with him, she was pregnant and in distress. I tried to help her, he says, I tried to calm her down, but it was obvious pretty quickly that something was wrong. I stand, move to my doorway again, he is standing at his door, hands clasped against the bars. Something wrong medically I mean, he says. Maybe shock, I don't know. But she couldn't calm down, she was leaning over the man and she was hysterical, clutching her stomach and screaming. I tried to tell her he was dead and that she needed to save herself. And the baby. He starts to cry. She was about six months pregnant. I held her hand, he says, I tried to calm her down, tried everything I could think of, though I don't think she realised I was there, but then I was ordered to move away.

What did you do, I say.

I moved away, he says, what else was there to do. I don't know what happened after I left, but I heard her screams for a long time.

David, I say, you need to be quiet. They will hear you. He

turns away. He says, they are watching television they won't hear, and anyway they don't really care most of the time. They will, I say, they will hear and they'll punish us. After I left her, he says, I noticed the crowd watching her, but they were scared to approach. I stare into the dimly lit corridor, at the black door of his cell opposite me. I knew the man was dead immediately, David says, I knew he was dead. She did too. I took his hand to feel for a pulse but there was none there. When I let go, his hand just fell to the ground.

He turns back to the door of his cell, peers at me through the bars. One minute he was running through the crowd, he says, and then he was dead. I think of him, he says, but mostly I think of her. After that, he says, after that I couldn't go back to serve, couldn't search another house or stand at another checkpoint. When the letter came, I told them I won't go, I told them it is impossible for me to go. I presented myself at the base and told them that I am a conscientious objector. That's why I'm here, he says. That's why. His life was not worth less than mine.

The prison is silent. There is nothing but me and David, regarding each other through the doors of our cells.

*

The sun was high in the sky when we said goodbye. Saleem disappeared suddenly, evaporating in to the humid July air. Take care of your foot, he said, and then, I'm here most weekends, come back some time, he waved his hand to indicate the grey water, the rushes, the last slips of mist disappearing into the blue sky. Already the sun was casting white flares of light across the lake. And then he was gone and the beach seemed lesser for his absence. I did go back, though at the time I thought I wouldn't, I went back and he was fishing on a black rock. He was often there when I went; there came to be a certain stability about his presence, the certainty that we would meet on the beach, and fish and talk, eat barbecued fish, smoke cigarettes; and other times we sipped strong whisky and discussed what was happening in our lives and in the country. He was always the same: easy, relaxed, occupying very little of the world around him, existing completely and wholly within that world. And other times, he brought the girl with him, Sahar, so that later she too became part of the place and our meeting there.

*

The rain has stopped, it's quieter outside now, the water drips from the trees. I listen to the sound of water receding, flowing into deep cracks in the earth, so that it slowly retreats, disappears until silence descends on the desert again, and I hear the first bird of dawn. I sit at my desk and think about writing; the night warden is sleeping somewhere, I'm too tired, I put my head in my hands. After a time I walk to the window and look up at the sky – there is a gleam of light there, a softer light after the rain, and the world smells clean.

Thank you, David, another voice calls. Thank you for sharing your story.

David is quiet now, the pen is before me, I pick it up and I begin to write, and the first warmth of the sun descends upon the desert, touching the world with faltering rays of light; it finds the tiny opening that is the window of my cell, spreads shy rays across my floor, onto the desk, onto the page that lies before me. I remember.

Chapter Fourteen

It is winter, you travel through the evening in your friend Lafi's car. He works the night shift in the village factory at weekends and he lends it to you when you are on army leave, so that you can go fishing. The evening is full of rain, gusts of wind rattle the car, plastering dashes of water across the windscreen. There are no cars on the roads, you drive with the window open so that the rain streams against your jaw. You like to drive with the window open in winter, the feel of the cool air against your face. The car is low on petrol; you navigate through the evening as it descends into night, the road is slick with water, through the wet mountains of Galilee, until you see the gleam of a distant petrol station through the gathering darkness. The beam of light glistens brighter as you approach, the petrol station rises at you through the night.

She steps out from the small shop into the wet yard, and approaches the car. The hood on her jacket is pulled up against the rain and she glances upwards at the long sheets of rain that reach upwards to the sky.

She leans in the window, there are drops of rain across her cheeks, yes, she says, and her voice is sparkling, soft and rich, what can I get you; you don't speak for a moment. She raises her eyebrows. You can fill it up, you say. She has a delicate face, and her black eyes are warm, her dark hair curls out from under the hood of her jacket, and there is a streak of it across her face. It is too late when you realise that you don't have much money, that you didn't want a full tank, she is already filling it. You open your wallet and count your money, and you see you will have enough, just about enough.

It's wet, she says. It's a wet January. She gazes up at the sky again and a dart of joy appears to descend upon her and rush through her, she holds her small hands out to the rain. Yes, you say, and you notice an older man, peering out through the shop's window, wiping away the steam that comes from his breath, frowning through the night. She follows your gaze, turns to him and waves, the gesture coming from deep inside her; he frowns back at her, raises his hand but drops it again.

She returns to the car window, tells you how much money it costs and you hand her the money – your allowance for the next month gone on petrol for Lafi's car. I'll bring you the change, she says, and she is serious again, her fleeting moment of joy has evaporated into the night, towards the stars that you cannot see but that are there, obscured by thick walls of clouds. She runs through the puddles, into the shop and when she appears again she is walking.

Your change, she says, and she looks right at you, your eyes meet, she reverts her gaze, glances back at the man who stands at the window, arm raised against the glass. Thank you, she says. You drive away from her; her back is turned to you and she walks towards the doorway and the light, halting to brush the rain from her face.

You discover the beach that night, it is dark, everywhere is dark, and there is no light from the sky; but when you find it you shine the torch around you, and you like its smallness and its symmetrical shape. You know that in the summer it will be hard to find, it will be quiet, not many will come across it, not many will have the patience to find it, placed as it is at the end of an immense drive of rushes.

That night you sleep in the car, the rain lashes at the window, and you think of the girl, the rain on her skin, the hooded face, and the smile. You hear her voice, the smile in her voice, and when dawn comes, you rise and you fish, the lake is black and angry; and later you sleep again, a real sleep this time, the sleep that did not come in the night descends upon you. You sleep in the midst of the thunder and lightning and the mountains, stretching around you, eternally.

You stop at the petrol station on your way back that evening. You don't have much money, just enough for cigarettes. The man is there, he tosses the cigarettes onto the counter and there is no sign of the girl, just a vague odour that suggests her earlier presence. You place the money on the counter, the exact amount, he drops it into the till; you linger there, look around, perhaps she will appear around the door, affirming her existence, but there is nothing, only the dripping of the rain outside, and the man begins to wipe the window again, maintaining his lonely vigil, gazing at the wet Galilee mountains.

Chapter Fifteen

November 15th, 1994

Dear Sareet,

Autumn again, it is often autumn when I communicate with you! What a magnificent autumn this year, the temperatures pleasant, and the hot Arabian winds, though unkind, have not contained their usual ferocity. Already I dread the winter, the rain and wind have caused me great trouble with rheumatism in the last few years, last year was particularly painful – I learnt to plan my gardens around what my body could manage, and this was a new experience for me, the years had not taught me to deal with my own body letting me down! People noticed of course and spoke about it; I overheard Hilda Rosenfeld complaining about weeds amongst the paving stones outside the dining room, and Yitzhak Levy made it his business to approach me one evening and inform me that he felt the roses outside the community clubhouse (an impressive building that was built after you left) could do with a more extensive pruning.

Never mind. The summer months were generous to me and I caught up with my work, though I am feeling a little exhausted this autumn; autumn is a tired season you used to say, but I never felt that until now. Dr. Cohen says that I am very young to be so afflicted with this rheumatism – perhaps it was those early years by the lake, the poverty of my childhood – who knows, he said, but life comes back to haunt us in many ways.

And indeed, after all these years, I have come back to haunt you once again.

As you may have guessed, none of the above is the reason for my letter today, I am merely rambling as always. I realise that the last time you wrote to me, after I refused your offer to return, you asked me not to contact you again, that in future any contact within our family will take place between you and Avi alone (amongst the many insults you hurled at me!). I have respected your wishes until now, but I want to share today with you. I realise that you probably still feel nothing towards me, only a dull contempt at my unwillingness to take a chance as you call it, though then again I like to think that the years between then and now might have softened you, you may have found your own peace.

I am writing to you today because I believe we need to put the past behind us, Sareet, and once we do so it is behind us forever. Because our son, Avi – yes, I am calling him your son despite the many ways you failed him – was sworn in to the Israeli Defence Forces this evening. As it happens I am just back from the ceremony, and I wanted to take the time to write to you about Avi's day, though I confess that in many ways I feel that it was my day too: for Avi is officially no longer my responsibility, Sareet; for the first time in eighteen years he is now fully the responsibility of another party.

I want to thank you for writing to him diligently over the years, in response to my request some years ago now, and for continuing to write, even after I decided you should not come back. Part of me believed then that you would cease to write to him at that time. Your continued letters have meant a lot to both of us, and it has meant that Avi has gained some sense of family, something other than me and his kibbutz peers (who of course are a family of sorts). I believe that your letters are very much part of the reason as to why he is such a strong, confident young man, and to why he was sworn in to an elite army unit this evening, in accordance with my aspirations all these years. He looked smart in his uniform: youthful, eager and ready to serve his people, and at the same time vulnerable and far too young to be undertaking such an adventure. I took some photographs and will send one on to you as soon as they are developed.

The ceremony took place in the Negev desert, in southern Israel. I am sure you remember the holiday we took in the south, that winter when Avi was a very small baby (how you resented vacationing in winter when there was very little work to be done in the gardens! And yet in the end you liked it – the rainy days, the sound of the rain in the desert, the dull thud of water against the roof when the three of us sat indoors playing cards or board games. And then there were the hot afternoons, sitting on the shores of the Dead Sea, watching the approaching black clouds, and the occasional flash of lightning over the mountains of Jordan). The place where we stayed is not far from here as it happens.

It was a long journey. Avi encouraged me not to travel, it being such a long way from the kibbutz and given that I have been unwell recently, but obviously I insisted on attending. I left early this morning, brought a packed lunch so that I would not need to waste time stopping in the heartless fast food restaurants that have sprung up on the roads here, beckoning the traveller with their neon lights and promises of steaming hot coffee. This country is very different from what it was when you were here; it has succumbed to cheap Western capitalism, perhaps this was inevitable all along.

After an hour on the road, I knew I had made the right decision in taking the trip for I'd forgotten how endless the sky in the desert is. You do forget you know, I am sure you can scarcely imagine it now, and I was glad for the opportunity to see it again. As I drove I was reminded of the northern skies, the grey January evenings of my youth, and I wondered about how I've never gone back; I wondered about going back, or coming back, whichever it is. I've never managed to decide.

Immersed in these thoughts my car wove its way through the orange desert, sputtering up the steep hills, towards great staring caves carved out of mountain rock, then plunging down towards the vast desert valleys, where riverbeds empty of water wind their way through the stone, great snake-like shapes where in winter the fallen rain hopelessly searches for the sea. Avi will spend much of the next three years in this place, meet new people, friends, comrades, and I was conscious of this throughout my journey. In many ways I gave him away to the desert, for he is an adult now and must make his own way.

Please don't be angry! Don't tell me that you should have been here, rage at me, write me another letter where your very anger explodes from the pages, declare your contempt for me for yet again informing you of an event after it actually occurred. You see, this was Avi's event, not mine.

I am sitting on the balcony of my hotel room. The breeze is warm, the palm trees tower above me, ghostly under the pallid light from the stars. Voices drift upwards through the night air, for even at this hour there are people floating in the sea. I shall stay here tomorrow; upon arrival I decided I would stay an extra day, for the days here are filled with life and blinding light. How alive I suddenly feel! Such a short time I spent in the desert, yet – now that I have returned – it seems that the most memorable moments of my life are filled with it: can you imagine how it was for me, a young chap from northern England, the eldest of seven children, fatherless from a relatively young age, who left school at just eleven though hungry for an education, for something to remove me from the simple poverty in which I spent my youth. Can you imagine what it was like reading books and articles about the homeland, the pioneers, the return, the kibbutz movement!

How I devoured the very words. And then the Yom Kippur war, finding the courage to leave home and travel there, discovering the kibbutz and leaving it again. Try to envision what it was like after leaving it, not knowing where I was going, to what frontier I would be sent, thought it scarcely mattered – for they were all unknown entities to me.

And then seeing the desert for the first time! The thrill of those days: the first time my pale virgin hands handled a gun, the power that was conveyed to me in one moment, the heat, sweating under the thick uniform, the convoy of tanks as we moved across the desert in unison, dust ballooning in our tracks. The smell of gunpowder and of the dead. The strangeness of the food, the painful diarrhoea and the tightness in the stomach on those hot desert days, followed by evenings filled with whispered plans and new resolutions under the starry desert skies.

And finding you.

How vast is the silence of the desert. How immense, the whispers of its breezes and its boundless silence, telling me that I know it, I've always known it. And yet how empty it is, so that all at once, on the night when I give Avi away to this place, there is sadness for things gone: your leaving, battles fought, won, lost, bodies that melted in the heat, hurriedly buried, thus remaining a part of the desert; the sand and the stone and the endless stare of the sun. There is sadness for those who died, even the enemy, for you cannot know what it is to shoot a man or to come across a fallen comrade, you cannot know anything about how quickly the body disintegrates, collapses into nothing. You cannot know the groaning, the manner in which it comes again, years later whilst asleep, the stench of wasted flesh splashed on your uniform, matted in your hair.

I do not feel inclined to sleep tonight, though my eyes are dry and red from lack of sleep and November dust. I shall wake early tomorrow, if I sleep at all, watch the dazzling desert sunrise, live again the moments I existed in the desert.

I will leave the day after tomorrow, weave my way through the desert, it's stone caves and endless secrets, past the sea. Do you remember the Dead Sea, how you floated on the water and stared at the desert sky for hours? It has receded, this sea, in fact it recedes more each year, succumbs to the rays of the sun; the land it leaves behind stares blindly, vacantly at the sky, as if it doesn't quite understand, as if it shall always await the return of the sea.

Many of us know what it is to wait.

Daniel

Chapter Sixteen

There are incidents people do not like to recall, almost impossible to speak of. It was morning, the sun already harsh against his eyes, so that Saleem raised his hand over them and watched me as he spoke. You don't need to tell me, I said. After all, I've been there. I know what these places are like, especially at night. No, he said, no, let me tell you.

You'd been to this place before, most recently on a rainy day, a day so wet that the excess water ran in streams through the saturated alleys that separated the makeshift huts. The women were huddled indoors throughout that visit, in their huts; they aren't houses, you said, they are nothing like houses. Have you been inside the huts there, you asked, yes, I said, I've been inside. So you know the smell there, you said, you can recognise the smell, that mixture of spices and squalor?

The children had made the best of that wet day, playing with old orange crates, pretending they were boats, using thin sticks for oars, and you smiled when you saw them for they were far from the sea, its tides and its fresh breezes. You patrolled the camp on that visit, up and down through the wet winding alleys, a cold gun in your hand.

You've been to this camp before, but never at night and never in this heat. For it was late spring, a time when the hot winds blow from Arabia; it was so hot, you said, it was impossible to describe.

Tell me what happened, I said, and you stared out at the lake and then you began to speak.

Your convoy travels to the camp in silence, crawling through the night with just an occasional splutter from the jeep, but they know you are coming, they know you are out there. There has been a bomb, and your orders are simple: it is known that the culprits came from that camp. You and your fellow officers have three names, your own orders are to catch one of these names. You look on them as names, and you believe these names know you are coming. There are signs: there is a dog barking in the distance, promptly silenced, there are lights that are distinguished against the black night, there are the black shadows against some of the huts as you approach, shadows that disperse into nothingness.

But your name doesn't foresee your imminent arrival into his home, his life. The jeep comes to a halt and you creep into the night, the cold metal of the machine gun against your skin, your finger against the trigger, ready to move quickly – you are taking no chances in a place like this. They know where the hut is, some of the other soldiers, they have been there before. They know these alleys, wind in among the huts effortlessly, until it becomes clear to you that one of the huts has been singled out, marked; and in moments there are soldiers on the tin roof, and the hut is surrounded. In the time it takes to blink, strike a match, take a breath, this small hut is surrounded by armed soldiers and there is no means of escape. And you, you are one of the soldiers who are to search inside.

I remember your voice as you described that room. You

began to describe it, but then it cracked, you lit a cigarette. Let's make more coffee, you said, and you turned away from me, and when you began to speak your voice was strong again. You placed your hand against the coffeepot to test the temperature.

I know those rooms, I said. There is no need to describe that room to me.

You don't know this room, you said.

They are all the same, I said. Whoever has served in the territories knows how those huts are inside at night. You looked at me, stirred sugar into the coffee, gazing into its dark depths. Perhaps you are right, you said. But I like to think that each home is individual, for individuals live in them, they have made them their own, despite everything. You poured the coffee, thrust a glass towards me and the rich fumes came to me in the heat.

It is the smell, the sharp smell of poverty. It gets you on the way in, and it closes against your throat, like a warm hand pressed there. You gag. Plenty of times, as a child, you thought you saw poverty, believed you had poor friends who had almost nothing. But you know in this moment, this smell, this smell that greets you on your way in, this is poverty.

You run into dead air, into the stench of sweat and nothing and hopelessness, burst through the door into their room – there are six people inside that room. They stay with you, these people, years later you remember their faces, you see them at night. There is an old woman, her face against the wall, she doesn't turn when you enter. She merely starts keening, weeping, her voice rising in a crescendo of anger, grief and fear. There is a child, a young boy who begins to cry and crams his hand into his mouth. There are two young men, mere teenagers, still dressed in their work clothes of heavy blue cotton, as if ready to arise and run to wherever they are told to go; sharing a wool blanket, the type that scratches the skin, they barely find time to raise their heads as you enter. And there is a couple. They stare at you in confusion, squinting into the light of your torch, and you know that they were making love, that they are still entwined, struggling to break free of each other, and somehow maintain their dignity. All this you see in an instant.

Though there is dirt on your shoes, you step across the blanket, towards the man, you know he is the one you need to catch, the man who only moments ago was making love. The woman is crying now, please don't take him she says, but you grab him by the arm, he is struggling with his trousers, and you pull him; there is a pounding on the roof from the soldiers that stand on it, you drag him towards you, he struggles against you, but he has no choice except to follow. You retreat through the room towing him after you, you stumble once and your hand rests on the sleep-warm blanket that covers the young boy, whose eyes are closed and whose face is wet with tears. He is only young this boy, but you see his future, on his face, carved there in that hopeless moment. Then you continue through the room, shoving the young man through the doorway, out into the night. The woman calls after him, but he doesn't turn and his back remains strong beneath your grasp.

You emerge into the night air – it is hot, the wind is full of dust, but it is fresh after that room. The prisoner comes with you, he has no hope of escape, he is surrounded and he knows it. Your fellow soldiers cover you, it is possible that this young man's comrades will try to rescue him, shoot at you and your convoy, so you do not relax for even a moment. You walk through the alleys, and presently a fog begins to descend, for it is still springtime, and the hot wind is lifting, the rain is coming. You raise your face to the sky, there are no stars now and rain clouds are approaching. You push the prisoner in front of you. Before you, a woman comes out of the doorway of her home, wiping the drops of rain that are on her doorstep with a mop – she raises her head to watch you and she is not afraid. She is the only other person on this wet street, besides soldiers, for the inhabitants of this camp now know there is a raid being carried out. She calls out to the prisoner, salutes him with her hand, and he responds; but one of the soldiers kicks him and he is quiet again.

After that you walk for a long time, into the haze of the night, away from the camp, you are waiting for a convoy to arrive and pick you up; exhaustion descends upon you, and nothing seems real, maybe because of this half rain that falls, the last rain of the season. The prisoner's back is warm against your hand, and at that moment, perhaps due to the absolute silence around you, broken only by the sound of footsteps and the occasional muffled cough, the light that shines off the wet road, the air seems free of enmity, fighting, war, and it is almost impossible to believe that the man in front of you is your enemy.

That place still lives inside you, you said, that night and the long walk and the gradual coming of the dawn, and the young man, he lives inside you too, you said. You don't know what became of him, but you remember his dark hair, and his brown eyes and the unique way he had of walking, the way he held himself erect, you said, the way he walked straight and proud, though he faced prison, captivity, the darkness of a cell for years; he walked tall and straight in the night, and you decided as you walked behind him, your hand against his back, you decided that you would ask the girl in the petrol station to marry you.

Chapter Seventeen

December 4th, 2000

Dear Sareet,

I am writing to follow-up on our phone conversation of last night, now that it seems certain that Avi will live. The last few days have been exceedingly difficult. I would like to thank you for your help and support at this time, and for your willingness, and indeed enthusiasm, to drop everything immediately and rush to Avi's side.

I understand your need to come and visit, that you intend to come anyway, even now that Avi will live, and I understand the delicate nature of the decisions you need to make, whether or not you should bring your other children. That decision must be yours alone, you must do what you feel is best, both for you and the children, though often, in times like this, the interests of the children are overlooked. I am not sure how old they are now, nor what they know of Avi.

I must advise you that Avi is deeply traumatised and perhaps I should explain to you, now that I have the time, the exact events of that evening. It was a Saturday, he came to visit that morning, we sat on the patio for a time and I smoked a cigarette, it was a mild day for early December and the sun was pleasant. I hadn't seen him for a month; he has lived in Tel Aviv for some time now, a different life from what we have here. Nevertheless he has adapted well to city life.

He did some chores for me, as you know I've had some trouble with the gardens over the past few winters. I brought him round the gardens and he climbed ladders that I find hard to negotiate, pruned my wisteria, the roses and honeysuckle (you will appreciate how unruly and out of control they become), and he did great work with the bougainvillea, though it's an extremely tough plant to prune. We ate lunch together before he left, he spoke about his work in Tel Aviv, his plans to travel next year, to the Far East, and then on to Australia. I told him that it's a good time to go as far as I'm concerned, for there is no denying that life is hard here, and people feel under siege, particularly in cities such as Tel Aviv and Jerusalem. Indeed I urged him to return to the safety of the kibbutz, I told him that he could have his pick of work: in the cotton fields, the orchards, or the factory. It's what you know, I said, you belong here, and besides it is safer, you'll earn a good wage, you're a good worker; but he shook his head and said that he likes Tel Aviv and city life, and though he feels the need to be careful, he does not feel under siege.

Well, who am I to stand in the way of Avi and his youthful plans. Why I was just a young man when I left my family, England, and all that I knew behind me, the forests and lakes of my youth, and left for a war in a country I had never glimpsed. You surely remember those times, Sareet, the hopes and dreams of our country weighed heavily on the shoulders of our armed forces, I know you felt it too: I remember the plane trip, touching down, the autumn heat – I had never before felt a hot breeze on my skin; the journey to the kibbutz, the volunteering, and finally the going to war, the victory, the coming back.

And I remember you, an orphan from Tel Aviv, adopted by the kibbutz after the death of your parents, our immediate connection, as if we already knew each other you said, the awe in your grey eyes, the pride and the desire, and the sadness, for it was a tough war with many losses, and the kibbutz lost too. Those young names, read out each year on the day cast aside for remembering, those names became a part of all of our lives in the years that followed, but for you they were already a part, for you knew them, the people who owned those names, you knew the loss of them. The comradery of that time still grips my heart! The never say die attitude of my comrades, the hot, endlessly long, never-ending autumn days, and the nights, the whispered plans, the waiting for dawn, and the cold that can descend on the desert at night.

Indeed, Avi's words brought that time back to me, vividly, as if it was yesterday. I don't feel under siege, he said, and when he spoke he faced the gardens of his youth, beyond them the sea he once made his own, and I watched his hand clench, he had placed it against the table, hard and brown, a hand that knew the sun, he clenched it into a tight fist. He didn't look at me. I must be going, he said, the roads will be busy.

The next time I saw him was in the hospital, in Tel Aviv. You will come here, see him for yourself, and yet I must prepare you somewhat for what you will find. Avi returned to Tel Aviv that Saturday, he met a girl, a friend from his time in the army, Hagar was her name. He met Hagar and they went to a restaurant, to drink coffee – it seems that this is a popular thing to do in Tel Aviv.

It was a busy night, Saturday is a busy night here in the towns and cities. It's only now as I write this that I remember that you, Sareet, are not a kibbutznik, indeed are from the city of Tel Aviv, you are familiar with the Saturday night ritual of 'drinking coffee'. Avi and Hagar went to drink coffee last Saturday night, they could have had no inkling of what was to come.

He does not remember much – don't worry I am not going to bombard you with gruesome images – what he felt at a particular moment, the red hot ball bearings searing into his flesh. I have not asked him and he turns away at the memory. I will merely give you the facts, unpleasant as they are: there was a bomb on the street next to where Avi and Hagar sat drinking coffee, they were sitting outside, that is important to note, for the fact that they sat outside saved Avi's life. There is no doubt about it, a bomb has much greater effect in an enclosed area, those who chose to sit inside that night are now dead. After the explosion people panicked, rose to their feet, called out to each other, what was that, was it a bomb, it has to be a bomb, what direction did it come from, and already there was screaming and the sky was bright. Avi says there was a siren very quickly, how quickly I asked, I don't know he said, but it surprised him just the same for it seemed to be straight after the noise.

The noise. That's what he calls it, he doesn't call it a bomb, or an explosion or any of the terms we use to describe such an event. The noise, he says, and then he turns away and fixes his eyes on the wall, on something he sees there, what I don't know, but he stares at the wall, and it is some time before he turns to me again.

So Avi and Hagar got to their feet, she was frightened this girl, she called out to passersby. What is it, she shouted, and Avi reached out to her but she continued to shout, what is it, is it a bomb?

People started to run, phoned the emergency services, their friends, parents, who knows what occurs to people in such moments. Others poured out of the surrounding restaurants and stood in the streets, calling to each other, but it quickly became clear what had happened, for the air was full of screaming, howls of agony, and sirens were ringing out through the December night. Which way should we go, Hagar asked Avi, she turned to him, clutched his wrist, which way should we go, Avi, she shouted, and in that moment another person entered the restaurant, a young man, moving against the people who were crowded around the door of the restaurant. Avi saw him, he looked at him, registered something but ultimately nothing, there was a child that he saw there, he had dropped his teddy bear and was reaching back to it, but his parents were pushing towards the door, and then there was nothing, nothing that Avi remembers, only that any last remaining person in the restaurant – those people who were making their way towards the door, gathering their belongings as people do in such moments, the boy reaching for his teddy bear, the boys' parents, the young man with the bomb strapped to his chest – was blown apart, the window blasted outwards, towards him, towards Hagar, and dozens, hundreds, thousands, who knows, who has a quantity for these things (other than the person who assembled the device, of course) of ball bearings and nails were streaking through the open space that once was a window, piercing his body at various entry points, weaving a path through his body, blazing through his flesh.

How easily the human flesh succumbs to these burning weapons. He remembers nothing after that.

After that, there is only what I've seen on the news, read in the newspapers, in the time I've had to watch the news and read the newspapers. After that, Hagar died, immediately, she never had a chance – her vital organs were severely damaged, and she went immediately into a deep sleep, out of which she never came; in fact she was buried two days ago.

I have not told him.

What do you say? Perhaps when you come you will help me to find the words and the manner, or perhaps I will already have found the courage to tell him by then, after all, he is conscious more often now, and he has started asking for her. I'm afraid I have not been particularly noble in this instance, I've turned away and pretended that I don't understand what it is he is trying to say. He tires easily, these conversations do not last for long.

I did not know her; she is a part of his life of which I know nothing. I do not know what she was, what they were, and therefore I do not know what he has lost.

If you could perhaps call prior to your arrival and let me know of your expected arrival time, I shall try to meet you at the airport. In the meantime, I have booked a guest accommodation for you on the kibbutz, an entire apartment in case you decide to bring the children. I wish you a safe journey and I will do my best to assist you upon your arrival here.

Daniel

Chapter Eighteen

It is your next army leave, the final one, for soon you will finish your three years with the army. Evening and, because summer is coming, the heat of the day lingers in the air, and the smell of jasmine is all around the yard. They have moved the chairs from the kitchen outside: Grandmother, Father, and Uncle Sabri, who is older now, his hair is white, his jawline thicker than you remember. They sit on the plastic chairs, and there is only the noise of your grandmother cracking sunflower seeds between her teeth. None of them speak. Occasionally Uncle Sabri springs up and examines one of the pieces of machinery in the yard, turning it up to the light, for the ground is covered with rusty instruments, parts of old cars, cracked flower pots, a dirty sink. Your father nods at you and you stand there for a time.

Your father lights a cigarette, he looks at you, gestures at you to sit, your eyes meet briefly, and you have an impulse to tell him that you are on your way to ask a man if you can marry his daughter, and perhaps he would like to accompany you. Somewhere inside you there is the awareness that other families would handle a situation like this in such a manner, and with your father by your side your request might appear more valid. It could one day be important to them, your people, this day, this moment, this very evening with the streaks of cloud trailing across the sky like tattered flags, surrounded by a blaze of red light. You recognise something of yourself in your father at that moment. You want to sit with him, light a cigarette, and talk about the petrol station on the road to the lake, the man at the window, the right way to approach him, did he already guess at your intentions. Grandmother cracks another sunflower seed between her teeth, spitting the shell in your direction, are you sitting or going, she says, and the moment is gone then. Father turns away from you, turns away towards a rusty hubcap that Uncle Sabri is holding in the air. He stands to examine it, then sits back down on the plastic chair so that it heaves beneath his weight. In the end you travel there alone.

*

Which daughter, the man says, I have nine daughters.

You stand in front of her father and you try to describe her to him. He watches you intently for a time, a crease across his forehead. He is no longer the sour man, wiping away the remains of his breath from a winter window; he is intense, avid, anxious to help.

I have nine daughters, he says. It could be one of three of them, they are of a marrying age, and they've all worked out there, he nods towards the yard. Never mind, he says, I will bring you to them, and you will show me the one. But first, tell me about yourself.

You tell him where she will live, that you are in the army, he blinks and nods, and it is as you suspected it might be, for he relies on Israelis for his business to succeed, an Israeli flag is discreetly placed inside the window of his shop. The arrangements are made, there in the shop, with the smell of petrol all around you, and the fat sausages that he tends on a stand rotating between you and him, the steam rising against his red face. In the end he nods and grasps your hand, I think it is the eldest girl you mean, he says, I am fond of her, but you seem like a good man.

He calls out to his wife in the house behind the shop, talks to her in urgent tones, disappears through the door, and you hear hurried footsteps, hushed voices coming from the house. The father emerges again, a bottle of Arak held to his chest, my name is Sulieman, he says, and he thrusts his hand towards you. He takes two glasses down from the shelf behind him, pours an equal measure into each glass, raises his drink to you. Drink, he says. Drink to my daughter and to you, Saleem. This is good Arak.

What is your eldest daughter's name, you ask.

Sahar, he says.

Her name is Sahar. The name roars around your mind, the alcohol burns inside you, and he laughs and pours another glass. She is beautiful, no? Oh, you are not the first man who has had an interest, but you are the first who asked. How can a man with nine daughters refuse such an offer? Tell me, Saleem, where will you work? What type of care will you take of my daughter?

After a time he leads you outside, along a gravel path to a garden, a surprisingly tranquil place, behind the petrol station, looking down over the lake. She is there, the girl, two of her sisters sit with her, you see immediately that they are sisters. This is the eldest, her father says, pointing at her. This is Sahar. They all turn to regard you in unison and, suddenly wary of looking at her eyes, you turn again to her father, yes, that's her, you say. You nod at the sisters, and they nod back, their faces frozen masks in front of you. You don't turn to Sahar, though you feel her eyes on you.

You sit with them for a time, the sisters remain also, there are few words. Her mother appears with a jug of mint tea, sweet cakes, she nods at you, smiles, and then disappears inside, and presently the other sisters drift away and walk around the garden, bending over to smell the roses that grow there, reaching out to touch the aromatic foliage of the hyssop.

Sahar rises to pour the tea, pushes the glass towards you. You sit at the table with her, her body is rigid, she stares at the lake and she doesn't speak. You watch her sisters in the garden, and a young child, still a toddler, wanders outside and leans against Sahar's leg.

This is my youngest sister, she says. You turn to her voice. I want to study, she says then, the words come at you in a rush. I want to study in a university. She doesn't look at you when she speaks, her eyes are fixed on the lake below her, even though it is dark now, almost indistinguishable, only visible to those who know it is there.

You rub your finger along the table before you. What is it you want to study, you say.

Literature, she says. I've always wanted to study Arabic literature. It is a dream for me. She strokes the toddler's head. My mother had nine daughters, she says. She turns to gaze out over the lake again, and there is the hum of a mosquito in the air near you. I want children, she says, but later, after I finish my studies. Not now. I don't want to be that kind of wife.

Then there is a great rush of doors opening and her family

is suddenly all around you. The father lines up the daughters, names their names, kisses each one as he says her name aloud; then there are other family members there, they eat and drink into the night, the sky is inky black over the mountains of Galilee. You watch the girl, the side of her face, her smile, the way she glances at you from time to time, turns away if she finds you watching. There are no more moments alone with her until it is time to leave.

You are dizzy from the alcohol, sleepy from the food. You stand to leave, shake hands with her father, he pushes her towards you. For the first time her eyes meet yours.

And then, at that moment, you remember your mother with a pang, you wonder how it was for her, her engagement night, her wedding, the emptiness of her new home. You have lived without her for many years, for the very house you live in is devoid of recollections of her, its occupants loath to mention even her name, it is as if she never was. You do not learn from your grandmother or your father who your mother was. You are not sure in that moment who she actually was, for perhaps your memory betrays you, so you no longer know who she was, for a memory can fall through the hands, become lost, obscure, nothing. You only know that there was laughter, and music, and that the house was full of air and light, it was a place of words, of adjectives, adverbs and explanations, not the common nouns uttered by your grandmother, the grunts and the sighs; and there were books too. This girl standing in front of you wants that, and you can give it to her. For the first time somebody has asked you for something that you can give.

You will study, you say to her, I'll make sure you study.

Her lips curl back and she smiles at you, and her eyes smile too, and you smile back.

Karim is sitting at the kitchen table when you reach home, he has moved one of the plastic chairs back in from the yard, he smells of fish from the factory where he works. He is smoking a cigarette, the blue smoke curls towards the open door and hangs in the still air before drifting out into the night, and in a rush of words you tell him that you are to marry, and that the girl, Sahar, will study literature in University. How are you going to pay for that, he laughs. I'll work, you say, I'll work hard so that she can. There's work in the factory, he says, and he exhales the smoke from his lungs as he speaks, there's plenty of work in the factory, or are you above that, he laughs, are you above the rest of us after your three years in the army.

You pause at the doorway, watch his face that is turned towards you, I'll take it, you say, I'll work there; and the words are like a kind of death to you and already the smell of that factory is crawling over your skin. He laughs then, a yelp of sorts, you're coming to work with the dead fish, he says. You mount the stairs, quietly, your footfall leaves no echo in the silent house, and you stand alone in the darkness of your bedroom. You regard the mountains outside the window, shrouded by shadows and darkness, only sometimes the moon breaks out from the cover of the clouds and then they gleam white and eternal, with dashes of gold throughout, just for a fleeting moment.

Chapter Nineteen

December 12th, 2000

Dear Sareet,

You must be home now, tired, I'm sure. Perhaps you are already in a taxi in Amsterdam, your cheek against the window, the rain falling in torrents outside. It is winter, cold.

Now the taxi driver is pulling up to your apartment (you laughed at my idea of the high-ceilinged house, with the large garden I once envisaged). I see you standing outside the apartment block, gazing upwards towards the fifth floor, a dim light glows inside, but they are asleep, the family. The light was left on as a mere courtesy, and bracing yourself you walk through the cold rain towards the doorway, into the elevator, home.

Perhaps you are now sitting at that mahogany table you described, a glass of sherry in your hands. You are quiet so as not to awaken the family, you are tired, the kind of tiredness that deep trauma brings, sighing now, rubbing the palm of your hand along your forehead, you are not ready to talk.

I am hopeful you have calmed down somewhat by now, that the rage inside you has somewhat dissipated.

I should tell you that, despite the insults you lavished upon me throughout your stay, I'm glad you came, and came alone moreover, without the children, that you came to see Avi without them, as I had asked you to come, his mother. I waited for the opportunity to tell you that while you were here, but the opportunity never arose. You were tired and angry, and you were gone so soon after arriving – five days, that's all you had with us – upon your departure your very visit seemed surreal, imagined, and it is almost as if you never returned.

Yes, I have fed the stray cat that you adopted, you have not lost your ability to attract stray cats (I confess that this pleased me), he is asleep in the far corner of the patio purring. In fact I think he has adopted me in your absence, at least he behaves in a manner that indicates he is fond of me, and when I return from my work in the gardens he is waiting for me at the door and rubs against my legs until I feed him (he even comes indoors from time to time). Beyond him is an olive tree, glowing golden in the light of the blood moon, and the fig tree that you said was doing poorly, though I feel it will survive. I have planted the bulbs that you kindly brought from Holland, stripped the sheets in the spare room of the house, where Avi sometimes sleeps and where you insisted on sleeping: it is as if you were never here.

And yet you were here, you came back! And while you were here I stumbled upon the realisation that though you once left this place, it never left you. It is still there, part of you, I can see it in your eyes. It never left you, Sareet. And this place is full of you.

You must allow your anger to subside; for it is unreasonable, misdirected and a waste of your energy. Of course, the years have changed Avi. How did you ever expect him to have remained the same? You must try to understand that though Avi doesn't need you, neither does he need me. If it's any consolation, Avi does not need you, me, or anyone and has not done so for a long time – your leaving gave him the kind of self-sufficiency that you always had, that you now resent in him. Try to admire him if you can for learning not to need you – for if he had needed you, there's not a thing he could have done about it.

Do you remember that night when you shouted and screamed at us, said that you couldn't take it anymore, us, anything about your life, that death was the only way out? You were peeling an apple at the time and you brandished an apple in one hand and a sharp knife in the other. Or the time that you ran away, simply walked away from the patio, disappeared into the evening and didn't return, until I eventually deposited Avi in the children's house where he went every night, though it was way before bedtime for the children and I read deep resentment in Yifat's eyes (do you remember she ran the children's house for many years?) and went to look for you. I eventually found you in an olive grove, down by the orchards. You cried until the dawn so that I knew you would leave eventually. We sat there until sunrise and eventually you came home to take a shower, and at breakfast I met Yifat and she told me that Avi did sleep that night but that for a long time before sleep came he stared at the wall, eyes open, perhaps his mother was already lost to him then.

Daniel

Chapter Twenty

Grandmother is not well. The words come down the phone, your father's voice, he barks out the bare details. He has never phoned you at the base before; you are surprised that they kept the folded piece of paper that you handed to Grandmother on your first army leave, in case of emergency, you told her, so that she snorted and shook her head.

The Army releases you immediately, out into the hot sun and the blue sky, and you travel back to your village by bus. There are three buses you need to take from the base to your village. You are surprised by the sick feeling in your stomach and the way your hand trembles. You lean back, your face against the cool glass, and you close your eyes.

The bus meanders through the desert, for you are far from Galilee with its winding hills and endless white mountains. You think about how she was the last time you were on leave. Father told you she was not well when you arrived that night; you couldn't see her as it was late, but you visited her the following morning. She was sitting in her room, the room that she once constructed to resemble her lost home, she seemed to have faded into the great chair, become part of it; yet her eyes were bright and the old sharpness remained in them, her thick white hair was pulled back into a bun at her nape, the immense strength within her was still apparent.

Saleem, she said in a whisper, and she smiled, so that you wondered had she become softer, had this sickness that descended upon her so late in life changed her. She sneezed into a small white handkerchief that she clenched between her hands. When do you finish with them? she asked. She sat forward in the chair, rejecting the support it offered, her face turned to the light that came in the window. Six months you said, six months and I'm finished. Good, she said, then she sat back and closed her eyes. She did not speak again for a time.

All your life you were scared of her. You looked at her hands that day, as you sat before her on the patterned couch, and you only saw in those gnarled claws the hands that once beat you, you saw the red-hot centre that was her palm when it lashed you across the face. You looked at her hard eyes, narrowing at the corners, and you saw the same eyes that had watched while your father beat you on account of her words, her version of events, your father who never beat you, only at her behest. She sat in front of you that day, your grandmother, erect in her chair, her eyes flashing at you.

Good, she said again, and you tried to love her, love her for her strength and her absolute faith in what she believed. You tried to love her but as you left the room you feared you would never love her, and now you are sitting in a bus, you are going to her and she is dying, you are sure she is dying, and you want to reach her, you pray you will reach her by nightfall because you want to tell her that you love her, love her for her faith and her beliefs and her crazy hatred. You don't hate like she does, you don't know how to, but you want to tell her that her hatred taught you how to love, and that even now you don't know that you love her, but you think it important sometimes that these things are said anyway.

It is late when you reach the village, the last of the daylight still sparkles in the west behind the clouds that roam far away against the horizon. You walk through the streets, nod to the people you know, they return the greeting, shake hands with you, whisper that they are sorry to hear that your grandmother is ill. When you reach your home you note that though the sun has disappeared, all the shutters are still closed against it. Your father comes to meet you, she is very ill, he says, she doesn't have long. We thought she would have gone hours ago. His hand is flat against your back, pushing you through the rooms, up the stairs, through to Grandmother. She's been asking for you, he says, she asks for you more than for anyone else, even her own children.

The smell of death meets you at the door, you know this smell, you turn away from it as the stench hits you, breathe it, before entering, nod at the rest of the family. They sit in silence, there is only Grandmother's heavy breathing. The shutters and the window are closed, making the room stuffier, darker, the smell of the very sick is everywhere. Only Grandmother's face and hands are visible, the shrunken claws that are her fingers clutch at the sheets, her nails are long and yellow, her breathing is heavy, each breath a gasp, a fight, and when it reaches her lungs there is a moment of triumph, a short-lived victory.

Saleem's here, says your father. He has arrived, and her eyes flicker open briefly.

You sit down, the seat closest to the doorway. Everyone sits there for a long time. Nobody speaks, you want to speak, you feel you should say something. There is a nurse in the room, she doesn't have long, she says, and she looks at your father when she speaks. She might not last this hour. She is busy around Grandmother's bedside, doing what she can; sometimes Grandmother coughs, a terrifying wheezing sound.

At thirteen minutes past three in the morning she speaks. She turns her face to you, words come out of the black hole that is her mouth. Tell them how we left, she says.

Grandmother, you say, and it is a question, for you don't know what she is asking. You lean towards her, her breath is foul against your face. We didn't pack, she says. Tell them. Tell them how we left.

Each word is a gasp, an effort. Yes, you say. Grandmother, you told us. We all know about it. Tell them, she gasps, tell them. You look at your father, he nods at you, and you begin to speak. You tell her about that day, leaving her home in the mountains, the pot of soup still bubbling over the fire, cabbage soup, fresh from the garden, spiced with her own herbs and her beloved rosemary, the fire still hot, the grief, the white chalk road in front of them, the heat of the day, the way the sun burnt their shoulders, the crown of their heads, the way your father cried as she pulled him behind her, the blisters that appeared on her feet, the agony of leaving. The plucking of some rosemary from the garden, rosemary for remembrance she told you, planted later in the yard outside her new home, under the jasmine and the weeping willow tree, so that every time the scent comes to her the remembrance rises in her chest in a great bubble of sorrow.

She dies, somewhere in the midst of your words, she dies, she loses her fight and gives up on life, but you continue for a time because none of you realise she is dead, and only when you finish the story, when the words drift away to be cleansed in the coming dawn, when there are no more words in the cooler morning air, no more events to add to that day, then the realisation comes. Your father drops his head and the nurse comes and leans over Grandmother, and when she turns to you there are tears in her eyes.

And you look at her body, fading rapidly into nothing and you know that nothing that she built here, nothing about this house, where she remained all these years, could match the home she once had, could equal what she'd lost when she lost her former home, for she lived her life with the knowledge that she couldn't have it again, could never have it again; and so it was not that what she lost was more beautiful than what she later gained in her new home, it was just that she had lost what she loved and nothing new was ever of equal measure in her eyes.

Chapter Twenty-One

Outside my window the line of cypresses lead away from this cell, down a grey, treelined driveway, towards the desert sky. I turn my face to the wall, it is visiting day, most of the other prisoners have gone to meet their families.

Zaki raps at the door. Avi, he says, you have a visitor. I turn to face him, the wind hurls the rain against the window. Who, I ask, and in that instant I believe it could be my mother, my heart lifts as it always does at the thought of her. Are you coming or not, he says, and then, it's that girl, the one who was here before. She came back.

I sit on the bed and pull my hands through my hair. Come on, he says. I have to get back. I go with him, through the dark corridor, into that room, it is filled with people, their faces wet, water streaming from their hair, surrounded by the pallid light that emanates from an unshaded yellow bulb, pale against the November darkness. As soon as I am inside I feel the need to contract, remove myself from people's gazes. I see David, his wife is there with two small boys, they sit with their faces towards the ground, wet hair slicked against their foreheads, an unconscious sadness upon their small faces, for their mother is angry, her voice is raised. Sahar is there, in the cubicle next to them, her hair is wet, and there are streaks of makeup across her face, I see that she has trailed wet footprints across the floor. Avi, she says, her voice filled with doubt, doubts that she has lived with for the past week, since I last saw her, they rise to the surface, I can see them in her eyes, she struggles to contain them.

Why did you come? I say. I thought you were not coming again. She turns away from me, rubs at an ancient ink stain on the rough wood between us, takes a deep breath that seems to fill her with resolution. There is another story, she says. I came to tell it to you. You should know after all.

Come home now, David's wife says, the children are here because they need you. One of the boys rises to his feet, reaches towards the corner of the cubicle, traces his finger along a spider's web, then plunges his hand into its midst. I can't, David says, patient, tolerant, I've told you, I will serve my time here, I have no other option. After that I will return home. The boys need you, she says. She strokes the back of the boy's head and he prods his finger through the web. You need your dad, don't you, she says to him, and she cuddles the other child closer to her. Don't do this, David says, don't do this, how can they possibly understand.

I run my hands through my hair. Another story, I say.

Sahar looks at me, our eyes meet, I read in her black eyes a determination, the uncertainty of last week has dissipated. Yes, she says, the rest of the story. She fiddles with the cigarettes she has placed in front of her. When did you start smoking? I say. I brought them for you, she says, and pushes them towards me under the gauze. I was thinking how unpleasant it would be here for you if you ran out of cigarettes.

What the boys understand, David's wife says, what they understand is that their daddy is gone. Darling, he says, I would be gone in any case, I would be in the Occupied Territories, carrying out work that is against everything I stand for. I cannot do that work anymore, he says. I will not do it, I've tried to tell you but you don't listen.

What are you talking about, Sahar, I say, why are you back here, what story do you need to tell me. Did the passport arrive, she says, I nod, and she leans forward, pushes her face against the gauze. She closes her eyes. The rain is falling against the windows, great driving sheets of water. How was the drive? I say. Her eyes cloud, I hate coming here, she says, it crawls inside me somehow and doesn't leave. She moves her face back from the gauze, her skin remains white where it was pressed against it. The drops of rain are drying on her skin. She looks right at me. You must listen, she says, you must listen to what I say, for it is exactly how it was. I turn to the great windows, the sky outside is oppressive, the cypress trees lead away to the hills, dark, darker even than the black sky.

*

My mother was content all through May and June, she sang to herself, smiled and laughed, as beautiful as she'd ever been. She awoke early in the mornings, made special treats for Father and me in the evenings, Yorkshire pudding that she said was an English recipe much loved by my father, and jam tarts, just like the ones her mother used to make when she was a child, and apple strudel, an old recipe of her grandmother's. She put makeup on one day, took the bus to the town, returned in the afternoon with shopping bags full. She chatted a lot in the evenings, made conversation with my father, discussed the gardens with him, and his vision for the future, expressed an interest in politics. She tidied the house, sorted through all my old clothes, brought them to the laundry where she said they could be donated to another family, placed my father's old gardening magazines in neat stacks on the coffee table, threw out old toys of mine and general junk that had accumulated around the house, polished the wooden table they had brought from the house in Tel Aviv after her family died, filled vases full of wild flowers that spewed their magic vapour around the house, so that every room was filled with an odour that was sweet and enticing and full of secrets.

*

Ienja came to the house one day. It was the afternoon, and I lay with mother on her bed, my face was to the wall. It was cool in the heavy heat of the day, mosquitoes hovered around our heads so that she sighed and waved her hands around in the hot air. She lay against me, curled against my back, her breath hot on my neck. There was a knock at the door, she froze for a minute against me, raised her head, rubbed her eyes. Stay here, she whispered, then walked to the window and peered out. Ienja, she said. She hurried barefoot to the front door, flung it open, and laughter drifted up the stairs, her laughter, its delicate notes like music, followed by a deep manly laughter. She beckoned him indoors, through to the kitchen, they stood for a time by the French windows, overlooking the patio that Father had lovingly tended over the years. He admired the plants on the patio, his voice drifted upstairs through the heat of the afternoon, and presently there came the sound of her making iced tea, the smell of mint, and I yearned to taste it, for the day was hot, but I did not move from the bed. There was something about the intensity of their whispered conversation that frightened me, and I dared not interrupt or intrude, though my body tingled with curiosity to see this man who made my mother laugh like a girl.

He didn't stay long, she ushered him out the door after a short time, you must go now, she said. And after he left she crept up to the room, her footfall silent upon the marble steps, she climbed into her bed and held me against her, fiercely, and I felt tears on my back, but I held my eyes closed tightly, so that she believed that I slept. After a time she began to read, she breathed deeply and turned the pages, until her breathing became calmer, or perhaps I just slept, for the afternoon became hotter.

Some weeks later I came upon the same laugh in the dining room, a Friday evening, and the kibbutz members and volunteers had gathered for the Sabbath meal. I heard the laugh, and turned instinctively; there was a group of men standing by the coffee machine, their backs to us, and I had no way of identifying the owner of the laugh. We had finished eating and people were lingering to talk to their friends. My mother heard the laugh too, she froze for a moment, before turning away from it towards my father and me. Gabi had joined us at the table, and they were discussing summer plants for the garden. Gabi was saying that people would like to see the area around the swimming pool being cultivated, and Father mentioned that he did not like a garden to become too manicured, and that often the secret was to keep an air of mystery about it, for Father still believed in mystery in those days. Later his gardens became more and more structured, but in those days he still believed that a garden was at its best when it withheld something from the casual observer, an air of secrecy or something that you could not find the words for.

My mother often referred to Ienja in her letters over the years, Ienja sends his regards, she would say, or Ienja has been wondering how you would look now; and I would remember him, or them, the dark-eyed bearded men from the dining room, their broad backs, the loud laughter and the warm smiles, the casual conversation between Father and Gabi, and the look in her eyes. If only I had understood it then, though perhaps I did, and I would see her there in his big house in Holland, for everything about him was big. I would remember her laughter in our home that day, how he made her laugh, and how she often looked at me, those melancholic eyes of hers devoid of laughter.

In July, her laughter and lightheartedness faded and a kind of despair descended upon her, she became broody and pensive. Or perhaps she didn't, perhaps I've unwittingly contrived to convince myself of that over the years. Perhaps a person can make an earth-shattering decision in an instant, maybe she really did wake one morning and decide to leave, and leave the same day, without an afterthought or a glance over the shoulder.

*

Sahar, I say, what story do you want to tell? Saleem's, she says, I want to tell you what happened. Saleem's, I say. But I know what happened. No, she says, no, you don't know. How could you know.

Her eyes meet mine and the smell of her is all around me, coming to me through the gauze, and for a moment it is summer in this shabby room. There is a beach, there is the heat of the day, and there is the sound of the water against the rocks. Saleem has gone to gather wood for the fire, we are there, Sahar and I, sitting on a rock, and her eyes that follow Saleem as he wanders along the rocks are so full of life and beauty that I want to kiss her. I lean towards her, Saleem disappears into the rushes, but she looks at me then, and there is nothing at all in her eyes, so that I turn away.

Chapter Twenty-Two

You blink to adjust your eyes to the dim light of the coffee shop. You often stop here on the way home from work, stop by for a cigarette and a glass of Arak. Mohammed knows what you will drink, and slams it down on the counter in front of you. Drink, he says, there is only bad news today.

You drink, the aniseed-flavoured drink burns the back of your throat, and you remain with your chin turned up, for you enjoy the sensation. Mohammed smiles, his yellow teeth glistening in the glow of the television. He turns back to the flickering screen, shakes his head and shrugs his heavy shoulders.

Ramallah, he says.

You turn to the screen, the men sitting at the bar are watching the images: masses of people on the streets, waving Palestinian flags, facing towards a balcony where men in balaclavas are dancing around in celebration, their hands red with blood, splashes of red and brown on their clothing, the bodies of two soldiers splayed across the road before them, encircled by the crowd.

Nobody in the bar speaks. Their drinking glasses are placed along the bar, fingers linger on half-empty glasses, the last rays of sun glisten through the years of grime that have accumulated on the windows. You watch for a few moments, and then turn from it, I'll have another Arak, you say, and Mohammed raises his eyebrows in question, for you don't normally drink more than one.

It's bad, he says, there will be trouble over this. He pauses as he fills your glass, gazes out the open doorway of his bar, it will get much worse now, he says, this is just the beginning. He is an old man, over seventy at least, his skin is wrinkled. Too many days in the sun, he says, his teeth are yellow and two of them have been pulled. Nobody at the bar speaks, they stare at the television screen with eyes that have seen this kind of thing before. Eventually the camera leaves the crowded Ramallah streets, the men with blood upon their hands, then people turn towards each other and talk in low voices, move away from the screen, until Mohammed raises the remote control and presses the mute button.

What happened? you say.

Lost, he says, they were lost. The words are stark, abrupt, his voice is hoarse and full of smoked cigarettes. Two soldiers on reserve duty, he says, they were trying to find their base and they took a wrong turn. Ended up in Ramallah. They were lynched at a police station. You saw the end of it.

Already he is turning away from you, for there is another customer at the bar, and around you the voices are raised again, murmuring to each other about what it will mean, and you order another drink, tilt your head back and feel the burning sensation in your throat, and sometimes Mohammed sits and talks and other times you sit just listening.

They walked to the police station, another person at the bar says. They walked in to ask directions. They never came out though, another voice says, and someone lights a cigarette, and someone else orders a Jack Daniels.

You light a cigarette and the smoke moves towards the windows, filthy in the dying evening light. You offer one to the man beside you at the bar, he nods in acceptance, places it in his mouth, raises the lighted match. Another Intifada, who knows, he says, and he shakes his head, like we need one, he says. And still, even now, it doesn't feel as if anything has changed.

Your legs are shaking when you stand up to leave and, instead of taking your car, you walk through the streets of your town. Nightfall has descended, an orange moon hangs in the sky, stark and vivid, and exhaustion hits you, for hopelessness is exhausting; people nod at you and you nod back but you don't see them, notice their faces or who they are. An Intifada. The man's words are in your ears, and you stand still as the full force of his words hit you, for you know just then, in that moment of tangerine moonlight, as the evening air embraces you, you know that things have changed, that nothing is the same, and if they are somewhat the same now, they will be less so in the morning, and even less so the morning after that. You lean against the wall, this wall at the end of the street, this wall that stood here through other wars, you lean against it until you absorb its strength; and presently you walk down your street, towards home, up the steps, past your father's house, and when you reach the door of your home, you don't go inside, you sit on the steps, and you put your head in your hands.

Eventually she comes outside.

Where have you been, she says, I've been worried. I was going to look for you, ask your father where you could be, I wasn't sure what. You move your hands away from your eyes, she stands in the doorway and moves towards you, then pushes past you, gazes down at the street, where is your car, she says, I did not hear your car.

Another Intifada, you say.

She pauses, you saw the news, she says.

You cover your eyes with your hands again, for the light of the moon is glaring and your head is throbbing.

Where were you, she says. Mohammed's? All this time? Is that where you saw it?

Things will get worse, you say.

Yes, she says, she places her hand on your shoulder, but this is not the first time, she says. It was horrible, she says, what they did. Did you see it?

Yes, you say, and she starts to cry then. You shouldn't watch, you say, you shouldn't watch images like that, it's too upsetting.

Saleem, she says. Saleem I'm pregnant. I just found out.

The world is quivering now, the moon is darker, almost red, pregnant, you say, and she wipes her tears, tries to smile, but it's a crooked smile, not real.

Yes, she says, I am pregnant. It was confirmed today. Her words come in a rush, I didn't want to tell you until I knew for certain. I know how you wanted this once I completed my studies.

You raise your eyes to her. Your eyes, she says, they are all red, Saleem, did you drink too much? What is wrong.

A baby, you say, a baby here, in this place, now, you wave

your arm in front of you, out towards the mountains of Galilee, beyond them the blood red moon.

Yes, she says, a baby. You are drunk, she says. Perhaps you should go to bed. She holds her hand against her stomach.

Slowly you get to your feet and stumble inside, towards the bedroom, the alcohol hits you now in a way it didn't when you were in Mohammed's. You fall forward onto the bed and you close your eyes, the room spins, you see the blood on the men's hands as they stood in front of the police station and waved them in the air, you see the brown marks of human flesh on their clothes, and you see the dead soldiers on the street, surrounded by cheering crowds, children with flags, mere boys laughing and leering. You don't want a baby, not here, not now, a child to ask the same questions that were never answered for you, that may never be answered, you know that now, for this goes on, much in the manner of a river overwhelming many streams along its way, overpowering them, until eventually they leave their own path and instead adopt the course of the river, the course that is carved out for them, the course that defines them.

The next morning you wake and your head is sore, she lies beside you, on her back, watching the ceiling, her hand on her stomach.

She does not turn to you; it's okay, she says, I understand. But life is always good, even here, even after yesterday. She moves away from the room to the kitchen, and then there is the smell of coffee, the sound of the spoon against the long glass. She brings the coffee to you, places it on the bedside table, sits down hard on the bed.

I'm sorry, you say. It's just we will need to be strong, we will need all our resolve to get through this, it will not be easy. A baby makes us weaker. That's all. For things will change.

She almost nods, barely, but you see it, you reach for her hand and squeeze it. I'm sorry, you say, it's just you have no idea what war is, what this might mean for us. It will be hard. You must be prepared for that. Everything will change now, you say, people will change.

It is warm that morning, hot and heavy, but you are aware only of the loneliness in the air, the cold that seems to penetrate everything, leaving a frozen weight somewhere in the region of your heart.

Chapter Twenty-Three

I observe the open doorway for a time after she finishes her story. That's how it was, she says; she is tired, she places her chin between her two hands. You have your own memories, she says, but that's how it was for us. Her eyes are filled with certainty; she has found strength from her story.

David's wife is crying. This is the last time, she says, this is the last time this family goes through this. She clasps a tissue in her hands and dabs it against her eyes.

Ruti, he says, Ruti, please listen. It's important, Ruti. She is fidgeting with the toddler who sits on her knee, reaching also to the other child, stroking his hair repeatedly, grabbing his hand, wiping the cobwebs from it, roughly, so that he screws his eyes up and tears run down his cheeks. She bites down hard on her lower lip. She shakes her head, no, she says, I don't want to listen, I am sick of listening. My father is angry that you are refusing to serve. The neighbours are asking me where you are carrying out your service this time, I'm tired of lying and pretending. Please do your army service, her voice is rising, louder, louder. He reaches his hands under the gauze, attempts to grab at her hands, but she pulls them away. He thrusts his hand instead towards one of the children, who continues to prod the cobwebs in the corner. He catches his chubby hand in his clasp, squeezes it hard with a kind of hopeless love that there are no words for.

A man got shot, he says. I was there.

Stop it, David, she says, stop it in front of the children.

There was a woman with him, he says, she was pregnant. My guess is six months. I remember you at six months. She places her hand against her ears, like a young child, and turns away from him, the boy on her knee remains staring gravely at his father. David roots in his pocket for his photos and leaflets. Don't David, she says, and there is a weariness in her voice, I've seen them before. I don't want to listen to any of it anymore.

He doesn't speak. She regards him, a terrible sadness in her eyes. I am leaving now, she says. I have my answer. Her voice is low. I will pack your bags and leave them at your mother's house. Please go there after you're released from here. Please don't come to the house. Her eyes fill with tears. Our house, she says, please don't come to our house. She is pushing the young boy off her knee, dusting down her skirt, fixing her hair.

Ruti, he says. Ruti. He stands up and leans against the gauze. His blue eyes have clouded over, he rubs his hand against them. Let me tell you about the territories, he says. We went into their houses, took over their homes. Searches, he says, always searches. She raises her hand in front of her face. And other times, he says, other times we would take over their homes, for days, sometimes weeks. We could do whatever we pleased there, he says, other than deliberately destroy their property, of course. As little physical damage as possible, as little harm to a person as possible, those were the rules, he says. But there were no more rules. Only those. He laughs, there are more rules here, he says.

She says, of course. It was just a vantage point, stop being so dramatic.

Try to imagine, he says. Try to imagine if they entered our home, not a police force, no warrant, but a unit of soldiers, imagine they burst into our home, shoved you and the children into the bedroom, frightened the boys, pointed their guns at us, emptied the drawers, searched through our belongings, your treasured things, even those things that you hide from me. He points his finger at her through the gauze. Try to imagine, he says, try to imagine you were doing that and trying to remain human.

She is reaching for her coat that hangs behind the chair.

I'm trying to be a decent human being, he says. Tell me that you could do those things and still feel like a human. Just tell me that, Ruti. Tell me that you could watch a man die, watch his pregnant wife clutching her stomach on a freezing street, tell me that you could abandon her under orders, leave her husband to die on the side of a street.

Ruti is buttoning her coat, reaching for the boys. Your jackets, she says to them, put on your jackets.

Just tell me that, Ruti, he says. Tell me that you could feel human and do those things. Just tell me that. Don't do this. You must listen.

She walks over to the open window, her back to the room, the cubicles, the voices, her face toward the darkness and the rain. I've heard it all before, she says. There is nothing else to say. It's a war and you are not fighting. She reaches up to her hair and smoothes it back from her face. You're behaving like a coward, she says. He flinches, her words strike him like a smack on the face. She turns from the darkness, looks at him. He pulls back and the colour drains from his face, she turns again to the darkness, placing her hands against the glass pane.

*

My mother came to the kibbutz when she was twelve, by then she was an orphan. There had been an accident, they were driving to Jerusalem, it was her mother's birthday. Three people died in the accident, her mother, her father and her little brother. My mother remembered nothing about the accident, nor did she ever speak about life before it, but she remembered the morning they buried her parents and her little brother as one of the defining moments of her childhood. She told me about it in one of her letters, she wrote about the sun in the sky, the heat in the graveyard, the smell of grief and dying summer lilies; she wrote of her brother's teddy that they buried with him, and how she longed for the bear in the nights that followed, longed to hold him against her and smell her brother. She remembered everything about that day, she said, the smell of the jasmine that climbed an oak tree not far from the graves and the wreaths of bruised white lilies that lay on the graves after they were filled in, and how, since then, she has loved the smell of lilies and jasmine, how she has surrounded herself with lilies and jasmine, always. She remembered the buzzing of the bees, she said, and the butterflies, there was a blizzard of butterflies before her when they buried her parents and her little brother.

She settled into kibbutz life with ease, she was young after all, there were many children there the same age as her, they welcomed her, this orphan, and the structure of kibbutz life suited that of somebody living with a recent bereavement. She was surrounded by fellow children all day, and at night slept in the children's house, along with her fellow teens.

She didn't feel their loss, not then, there were too many new objects around her, too much novelty. There was a swimming pool that she could swim in every day, there was a tennis court, there were long summer evenings. Her days were full, so full, that her nights were spent in a deep dreamless sleep. The loss came later, much later, she said, it hit her with the force of a hammer one night, in the depths of the night, it was dark and there was no moon. She awoke and she realised that the children who slept around her, they had somebody, were part of something, whereas she was alone, there was only her, and outside there was only the night. It grew inside her, this loss, like a small piercing that became a great gaping hole, so that by the time I was born, she said, it had almost exploded around her.

I'm only telling you this, she wrote, so that someday you will understand.

*

Sahar is watching David, her dark eyes fixed on him, transfixed by his conversation with his wife. Her mouth moves, but I can't hear the words, so that I have to move closer to her. Who is he, she whispers, who is that man. His name's David, I say. He's the occupant of the cell opposite mine.

What is he talking about, she says, who did he shoot?

He didn't shoot anyone, I say, he was just there when it happened.

She is pressing her nails against her cheeks, leaving white marks against her skin.

It didn't change you, I say. Not in the same way that it changed us.

She is the same girl as that girl on the beach, the first time, and all the days there that followed. There is the same quiet sensuality in the way she moves, her eyes are harder, the lines around them deeper, but her movements are just the same.

We've all changed, she says. We had to. She looks at David, at his wife and the children. First I must tell you more, she says. For soon I must leave. And you need to make your decision. You need to decide to help me.

The rain is falling gently and steadily, shimmering through the weak artificial light of this room, filling the grey light with its soft sound, while the evening invades the room step by step. She takes a deep breath and begins to talk.

Chapter Twenty-Four

It is a cold day, cold even for January. Friday, the supermarket is packed, so that you feel regret rising within you for coming here. You weave your way through the crowds, determined only to buy what Sahar has requested and exit. People push their trolleys towards you, against you, you move through them, twisting in and out between the trolleys, a handful of random items in your hands.

He is in front of you – Avi – he has changed, some fundamental part of him, you observe that immediately. He has been wounded, a bandage covers his left cheek, some of his hair has been shaved off, and beneath it there is a pink scar, still raw, snakelike, beginning on his cheek, then running along the side of his head. He stands in front of you, leaning against his crutches, his right leg covered in a plaster, black scorch marks cover his face, and meet in great clusters on his left hand and cheek, and all across his forehead. But it's his eyes that have changed. There is a man beside him, perhaps his father, fair-skinned, a man who holds himself erect at all times; his eyes move rapidly between you and Avi, settling on you for moments at a time before flicking back to Avi.

Avi, you say. He nods at you. The older man turns to him, a question in his pale eyes, but Avi does not meet his gaze and the man turns away, opens a box of eggs and examines the contents, discarding it, and opening a new box, peering at the eggs contained within. Sometimes he holds an egg up to the light, twirls it around between his fingers, and in the end he begins to move the eggs between the boxes, assembling them carefully until one box contains the six eggs that have met his approval. He stands in front of Avi with the box of eggs in his hands.

What happened? you say.

Avi glances at the other man. Is that your father, you say, yes, he says, but makes no move to introduce him, then picks a cucumber out of the trolley in front of him, holds it in his hands. A bomb, he says. About seven weeks ago.

You take a step back. He stares at the cucumber, does not raise his eyes to you. His father pushes the box of eggs towards him, put these in the trolley, he says, I am going to buy the meat. Avi takes the eggs, holds the box in his hands, opens it, examines the speckled eggs inside. He picks one up, holds it in his hand, it fits perfectly in his palm.

It was one of three in the same evening, he says, about seven weeks ago. Maybe you remember. He raises his hand to his head, runs his fingers along the scar. There are people moving around you, brushing past you. A heavyset Moroccan woman drops a bottle of wine, it shatters with a bang. Avi jumps, his eyes flicker alarm for an instant, and the red liquid spreads out before you in a great puddle. You don't move, don't speak, it feels like you don't breathe, but you do breathe, you are aware that you are breathing and he is breathing but there is no sound, the silence between you is absolute.

A man pushes forward, pressing his elbow into your back so you move backwards, away from Avi. Hey you, the man shouts at the Moroccan woman, he points his fingers at her eyes, hey you, you need to find someone to come clean this mess up, what do you think we are, animals; but she is turning away from him, pushing her trolley in between two women who are talking. Listen lady, the man shouts, who do you think you are leaving this mess behind you?

Where was the bomb, you ask, you raise your voice, for he hasn't heard you, where was the bomb, you say.

The first bomb, he says, the first bomb we just heard, it was nearby. And as people fled the scene, another one was detonated. A bomber ran into the restaurant where we were drinking coffee.

Tel Aviv, you say, I remember. It was in Tel Aviv. He doesn't answer, the red wine spreads across the floor, towards his plastered foot. Why were you there, you say?

I was drinking coffee with a girl, he says, a friend from the army.

He stops talking. He begins to wheel the trolley and you walk beside him, he leans on the trolley as he walks, putting little weight on his injured leg. We were talking, he says, she was laughing, and when we heard the blast we joined the people running from the scene, masses of us running up the street. It was night and some of the lights had gone out, and there was confusion everywhere. He stops talking, his voice drifts away, a woman pushes her trolley against him, he flinches, pulls back.

I remember that evening, you say. The bombs.

I saw one of the bombers, he says, he rushed past me into the restaurant. His eyes rest on you, but they are somewhere else. It was that bomb that got me, he says, the second one.

There was another one afterwards, he says, as the rescue services arrived, but I don't remember that. I was unconscious by then.

He begins to wheel the trolley again and you see his father coming towards him. You begin to back away, you feel that he is accusing you of something, what you are not sure, but his eyes are darker, sadder, more knowing than before; and the man with him is moving towards him, reaching his arm out, placing it beneath his elbow in a gesture of support. We should go home, he says, you need to rest.

Just then it seems to you that the world you stand in is his, the supermarket, the mall, the town, all creations of his people, and that he belongs to it, absolutely, and it to him.

I need to go, you say, I need to go now. He turns his maimed face towards you, and in that instant there is nothing left of the man you met on the beach that hot July day, the man you made your friend, the man you talked to about the past, your past, the man who gripped your hand before you left that first weekend. You know about these wounds, the agony, the nails tearing through the flesh, the damage that even one nail can do, the burning ball bearings, the slow course of the healing, the long dark days, for a body so burnt cannot go out into the sun.

Sahar, you say, Sahar is expecting a baby, maybe you will come and visit us, she would love to see you, but he is staring at the ground. Your voice trails off and you begin to turn away from him.

Your wounds, you say, how bad are they – you aren't looking at him now, for there is a part of you that can't.

They are getting better, he says, but the woman I was with was killed. There is nothing in his eyes when he says this.

I'm sorry, you say, and he nods, but you don't see him anymore, he is a blur. You come out of the store in a rush, discarding the shopping you carry in your hands on the shelves inside the door. The light outside is dull, and the air seems muffled, it is cold; something brushes against your cheek and you hold out your hand – it is snowing. It is the first time you've seen snow. You stare at the sky and the thin white covering on the shivering earth. You walk towards your car, bend towards it, touch the snow, feel it, crunch it in your hands, rub it against your cheeks. You stand by your car and you brush the snow off and mould it in your hands.

A cat springs from a skip howling, and you jump back; its mouth is open and it is screaming, and on its side is a gash, deep and red and raw. You sit in your car for a time and then you drive, slowly, for it is snowing. You don't wipe it from the windows, you let it fall against the windscreen, the starlike flakes melting against it, disappearing, becoming almost nothing but a drop of smudged rain on your window.

Chapter Twenty-Five

You remember that day, of course, Sahar says. I stare at the packet of cigarettes, yes, I say, I remember.

Will you bring me to England, she says, and she does not meet my eyes. She reaches her hand towards a large flower-pot beside her, placed exactly between my cubicle and the one beside it, toward the distorted stems of cacti reaching out in all directions.

Ruti is gathering the children to leave. She bends over the smaller boy, grabs his hand and waves bye bye for him to his father. Ruti, there is something else, David says, there is something else, there is integrity, there is gentleness, there is beauty. There is goodness. If you stay with me I will show you. He looks at the boys. I will show them, he says. I will show them, for they will see enough ugliness if they have to go where I went. He is standing and his voice carries across the room, so that Zaki and the warden at the door turn to stare at him.

She grimaces. Stop it, she says. Leave it now.

He stands there, a well-built man, not tall, the same height as her, his blue eyes flash at her, pleading with her not to leave. He looks around him, desperate for someone to back him up, add credibility to his words, the statistics are gone from him now. He gropes blindly towards me, Avi, he says, she is leaving, she is going, what will I do. There are tears in his eyes. He bends towards the cigarettes in front of me, fumbles with the plastic packaging. I take them from him, remove the packaging, hand him a cigarette. Ruti is at the door, she turns back, he signals to her with his cigarette, wait, he says, but she is gone then, all that remains is one of the little boys, he stands in the doorway looking back at his father, and then disappears after his mother. David sits again, pulls his chair closer to us, casts his eyes downwards, he sucks on his cigarette.

*

A few years after my mother left, she sent us a photograph. This is your half-sister, she wrote, her name is Iseult. I looked at Iseult, held her photograph between my hands. A brown-eyed child with dark hair that curled just like my mother's. He was there also, or so I had to assume, the man with the laugh, Ienja. I examined every last detail of the photograph: Ienja in a huge sweater that seemed too big for him, one of the dark bearded men from the dining room, raising a cigarette to his mouth, a tiny stub of light between his enormous fingers. There wasn't much to see: a man who was not particularly memorable, striding through the snow wearing just a sweater and jeans, squinting into the winter light, the child rolling a snowball, staring up at him, laughter in her eyes. And my mother, standing beside them, a vacant smile on her face. She was wrapped up in a heavy duffel coat, her face almost covered by a woolly turquoise cap, and she wore mittens and a scarf that matched. Her face was blue with the cold, her lips a thin streak, and she looked tired and anemic in that snowy landscape. She didn't look at Ienja and the child, or at the camera – she gazed instead at some distant spot. After a time I pushed it towards Father, who was sitting at the table drinking a cup of coffee, a gardening book open in front of him. He regarded it for a time, then pushed himself upwards, reaching towards the uppermost shelf on the kitchen cupboard, he placed it there, between two of my mother's plates, so that you could just see the child. The man was obscured by the edge of a plate, and my mother was not visible at all.

I would examine the picture sometimes when I was alone in his house. I came to know it so well that I could see it in my mind without holding it in front of me. Whenever I wanted I could envisage her before me, the thinness of the face, the blue lips, the distant eyes. There was a look on her face that I found mysterious, as if she didn't belong with those people at all, Ienja and Iseult, there was something about her stance, the way she gazed into the distance, that separated her from them absolutely. Then I would hear footsteps on the patio and I would rush to the chair, stand on it, reach upwards to the uppermost shelf of the cupboard, and thrust the photograph back between the plates.

The photo remained there between the plates, but eventually I ceased to examine it; and over time it was pushed further back, so that the child too became obscured, and eventually disappeared, and just a corner of snowy landscape was visible. Years later I remembered the photo, and reached behind the plates, but it was gone, and my fingers instead landed on layers of accumulated dust.

She never sent another photo, my mother, though at times I supposed that perhaps she had, only that my father had learnt to intercept the post.

*

David's cigarette has almost burnt out, he holds it to his parched lips. We've been together since we were sixteen, he says, me and Ruti. He turns towards Sahar. We've been together forever, he says. He takes another cigarette from the box, lights it off the cigarette he was smoking.

She nods, then turns away from him, towards me. I must go soon, she says, we are nearly out of time. She glances back at Zaki and he points to his watch.

Chapter Twenty-Six

It is early February, the air is cold, the house dark. Sahar doesn't turn the heating on, or the lights, she is too sick, she forgets, she says, she doesn't feel cold. You stand before her, it is evening; she turns to you and regards you, her eyes black against her white skin. Change your clothes please, she says, I can't stand the smell of the fish. She shudders.

The heating, you say, why don't you use it, you have to try to remember. She rubs her hands against her arms. I forgot, she says, and anyway I am not cold. She turns away from you, your clothes, change them please, she says.

After your shower you approach her, stand in front of her, so that her eyes fall on you. She is not having an easy pregnancy, the sickness never leaves her. The vase, you say, I want to bring it back. What vase? she says. It is on the table, you nod towards it, her eyes follow your gaze, she looks at you, why, she says, why now? All of this, you say, all of this that's happening, I want to give it back, I want it to be back in that house. Will you come with me?

Yes, she says, I will come with you. She splashes cold water on her face so that the colour returns to her cheeks, runs the hairbrush through her hair, it shines ebony black. You pick up the vase, almost without moving, reach your hand towards her, her hand is cold against your skin, but it remains there, and you clasp it gently, so that you almost don't feel it.

You drive through the darkness, the same road you drove with your grandmother as a child, for you have never gone back, it is just the same: the white chalk dusty road, carved out of the mountainside leading to the house, the same sturdy door, the olive tree, glowing silver in the February night, the weeping willow trees, three of them to the right of the house. A dim light glows from the room where you sat with the Jewish woman, the light just visible through the vast darkness where you and Sahar stand. Below you the lights of distant Galilee villages glisten like raw diamonds. The view, Sahar says, what a view. You knock on the door, the same sound all these years later, ringing out into the night, an intrusion into the regular noises of a Galilee night, the same footsteps approaching the door. Who is it? she calls out in a low voice. You don't know me, you say, at least we met only once, you may not remember. I have something I need to return to you.

What is it? she says, as the heavy door opens in front of you, and so it is you find her once again, standing in the doorway, as she stood once all those years ago, the same face, the same eyes. The years have taken a cruel toll: the skin is no longer young, the hair grey, there are tired creases across her forehead, and a certain madness in her eyes. She doesn't look at you but at the vase in your hands, her eyes rest on it, until she raises them to regard you – you are that boy, she gasps, the little boy. You nod. Her lips curl at the corners, twist into an ugly grimace, an effort of a smile, but her eyes remain remote, guarded. She glances at Sahar and back to you, I gave you that vase, she says, I don't want it back.

Take it, you say.

Why now? she says; she looks behind her, into the dark hallway, come in, she says, come inside. She turns back into the hallway of the house and you follow her inside. She pauses before entering the room where you sat that day with her and Grandmother. It's different now, she says. I'm sorry, you'll notice it is not the same room.

You follow Sahar inside, the Jewish woman leans against a table, not the same table that rested here before, it is not by the window, it has been placed against the wall, where the couch used to be, the couch where Grandmother sat that day.

After you came I changed it, rearranged everything, she says, it is not the same room you remember, I changed everything. Sit, she says, and there is no couch this time, there are three leather recliners surrounding the fireplace.

You must see there is no place for your vase here now, she says, the words tumble from her, it is not the same as it was. What can I get you to drink? Sahar shakes her head, nothing, she says, I don't want anything at all. The Jewish woman turns to you, not Coca-Cola this time, she says and there is a smile in her voice, but her face is sad, crazed-looking, and her eyes are distant. You shake your head, nothing thanks, you say, and she sits then, as if relieved. With trembling hands she reaches for the packet of cigarettes placed in front of the fire, and lights one, leaning back in her recliner.

Your grandmother, she says. Dead, you say, dead for some years now. I'm sorry, she says. She raises the cigarette to her mouth. I often thought about her, she says, I often wondered if she would come back. She leans forward in the chair, moves her hand towards you and the cigarette is close to your cheek, you can feel the heat against it. I believed for a long time that she would come back, that perhaps she needed to, she says, but then the years passed and she never did.

Can I leave the vase here, you say. Why, she says, the past is the past, that's all it is, it's only a room, she says, a house, bricks and mortar. My husband, she says, my husband passed away three years ago, and my son is dead, he died in Lebanon five years ago. Blown to bits, she says, and she laughs, a harsh, humourless sound. The ironic thing, she says, and she moves the cigarette against her mouth and holds it there. You watch the ash dangling in front of you, you know it will fall and when it does it brushes against her thigh, but she doesn't notice. The ironic thing, she says, is that I have no one left, there is no one left for this house. She rubs her thumb against an ash stain on her black trousers, there is no one left for this house, she says. What do you think about that?

You finger the vase, stare at it, the way the colours merge against each other, and then you lean back and place it on the table. You must drink something, she says, but you shake your head, all those years, she says, I kept that vase, I kept it because I felt I should, because it seemed to belong, not because I wanted to. I never particularly liked it.

But you really must drink something, she says, and in a rush she departs from the room, returning with three glasses of sherry. Sahar shakes her head, raises her hand to her nose to block the fumes from the alcohol.

The sherry is sweet, the fire is warm, the heat drifts towards you and you see that Sahar has closed her eyes. I'm sorry about your son, she says to the Jewish woman, and the woman smiles and nods and throws her cigarette in the fire where it burns brightly before disappearing in the flames. She raises the sherry to her lips.

We must go, you say, we will leave the vase here, she nods, if you must, she says. You drink the sherry in one gulp, rise to your feet and reach your hand to Sahar. There is nothing for this house the woman says, if there ever was any happiness here it died with him, my son, there is nothing now. You leave her then, staring into the flames of the past, the house and her own private tragedy. Sahar's hand is warm against you, I'm glad you brought it back, she says, it is nice to leave something behind that belongs there now that it has changed.

You walk out into the cool night, it is clear, and the view is before you, around you, you breathe it, she breathes it and squeezes your hand tighter, the view that Grandmother could never recreate, you say, and she cries then, Sahar, she cries and you hold her against you, behind you the woman, the Jewish woman, stares into what remains of her fire and you believe in that moment, perhaps just for that moment, that there is a certain grace in going back, in facing up to things.

Chapter Twenty-Seven

When she has finished her story, a silence descends amongst us and David looks away, towards the windows, and continues to smoke his cigarette.

She rummages in a scarlet leather bag. The ticket, she says, and she pushes a plastic package under the gauze. The words come in a rush, it's for you, Avi, she says, the ticket to London. I open the package, stare at the print. Seven o' clock, she says, next Thursday evening. I'll be there at half past four. I'll wait for you in the main terminal, outside the bookshop. She raises her eyes to me, daring me to be there, and I see then that the confidence is gone, and her eyes are again filled with doubt.

And if I'm not there, I say. If I don't come?

She resents the question, scrapes her chair backwards along the ground, opens and closes the clasp on her bag. You want to know how he died, don't you, she says. I saw it in the newspaper, I say. The newspaper, she says, and a coarse laugh escapes from her.

But first, I say, if I don't come. What happens then?

She raises her eyes to mine, and they are dark, there is just a shimmer of light in them, but panic too; she finds it difficult to think about this, what happens if you don't come, she says. What happens. She rubs her finger along the length of the wooden pane that separates us. What happens is that I go home, she says. She turns her face away so that

I can't see her eyes. I will wait until six, if you are not there by six, I will go home; in any case we'd never make it through security at that stage, and the weight of the world is upon her shoulders when she says this, but then she raises her eyes to mine and they are full of the consistency that is her, brimming with resolution.

Karim will marry me, she says. She shrugs and I see her returning home with a heavy heart, settling into the solitude, somehow managing to tolerate her life, abandoning her tales of study in Tel Aviv, her Thursday trips to the prison, a kind of certainty absorbing her over the months, years, the certainty that old age would descend upon her, slow and relentless. I could imagine the marriage, to a man she loathed, the slow suffocation, a marriage lived out in the very home in which she had found such happiness. I saw her again on the beach, the vitality in her eyes, and I saw the life ebbing out of them, slowly over the months and years that followed, the dust of all the summers, the heavy air, the weight of her grief.

And after that no more lies, she says, no more stories about studying. She holds the box of cigarettes to her lower lip, it turns white. If you don't come, she says, if you don't come I'll face up to my life.

She stares at the clock. I don't have long she says, and there's more to tell. She looks directly at me. That night with the jackals, she says, jackals know about survival. I look around me and she is the last of the visitors. They have helpers who stay on with the parents after new cubs arrive so that the family will survive. Did you know that? I don't speak, I take a cigarette and I light it. After all, she says, they live in such a harsh place. What else can they do?

There is the ticket in my hand, and she is before me, Sahar, this girl who found me here, discovered me, who sought me out in this place full of nothingness and broken people, I breathe in her beauty and the open-hearted passion for living that is hers, the instinct she carries inside her to survive. I marvel at her ability to leave: to gather her belongings and leave her entire world behind her, and her belief that the dead simply slip from the room and tiptoe softly away, closing the door apologetically in their wake.

I stare at the grey oppressive sky, and I feel the night that lives inside me bubbling to the surface, dragging with it the knotted mass of roots accumulated over the years, attaching me forever to this boundless land, the years that I've spent here, and more than that, my father, the white hills of Galilee. I remember everything about it all at once, or so it seems: the despair and solitude of my childhood, the homely smell of the children's house where I slept at night with my peers, the whir of the fan in the darkness, the click of Yefat's knitting needles when I awoke in the night, the stench of the crowded chicken coops where I was forced to labour one burning summer, the thick heat of the orchards where I toiled other summers, the sweet heavy taste of the apples that grew there, the delicious cold water of the irrigation system on the kibbutz, the cool perfume of the honeysuckle that descended every summer evening in my father's gardens, the smell of salt that lived on my skin through all those summers, summers of sweat and dust and football, but mostly the sea, the odour of earth on Father's hands. It all bubbles to the surface, overpowering my senses and it seems impossible to leave.

*

My mother came back after the explosion. I was in hospital, she arrived while I was sleeping, so that when I awoke she was there, beside me, her face hovering over mine, her finger raised to her lips, her forehead creased in great frowns of concentration. I didn't acknowledge her presence just then, drifted in and out of sleep, and each time I opened my eyes I was again surprised to find her there; yet the fact that she was there, her very presence, exploded through my senses. In the end she stayed for five days, she sat by my bed most of that time, brought magazines and books with her, flicked through them.

Occasionally she would place a magazine on her knee and stare in front of her at the wall, and she would begin to talk, she talked a lot when that happened, she seemed anxious to fill the room with the sound of her voice, though a gradual realisation came to me, the realisation that I didn't know who she was anymore, nor she I, that the years we spent together had left no trace on either of us so at times it seemed that we were strangers, and that the letters we had exchanged over the years had done little in the process of enlightening each as to who the other was. There was an awkwardness too, whenever her hand brushed against me, or once she leaned forward and her hair fell across my face, we regarded each other then and she moved away, and scraped her hair back from her face, binding it harshly at her nape. And other times she would stare at my wounds and reach her hand out, as if she wanted to touch them, as if that touch would become a kind of balm, but at the last moment she would withdraw her hand and stare out the window, or at a magazine. Yet at times I could still detect traces of her through an unconscious smile, an inadvertent sigh, a silent moment; at times I perceived in her voice the person remembered all these years, who I had once adored and who had known me intimately.

But it was like seeing a face in an immense crowd so that you had to walk through the crowd to reach that face, and it would blur with the crowd; and when you reached the point you thought the face had been, you saw it somewhere else and had to move towards it again. And it seemed to me that all that was left of her was her laugh and her smell and those quiet moments that belonged only to her, and lying in bed I wished that she would leave so that I could again return to memory. Don't you remember how it was, I wanted to say to her, but I would look again at her eyes, staring hard at a glossy magazine and I didn't find the words.

*

And if I leave, I think, what do I lose, what part of me drifts away, is left behind, will I find it again, or will it forever be lost in the immensity of this place. Like my mother, will it become an elusive part of me that is lost, though at times there is a whisper of something, a reminder, a smile or a laugh so it seems that it was never really gone, until the next gesture snuffs it out completely, so that it is obliterated from the minds of those who remember forever.

Sahar places the cigarettes before her, David reaches under the gauze and takes another. He hands me one and I hold it delicately between my fingers.

Tell me, I say. I want to know what happened.
She takes a deep breath and begins to talk.

Chapter Twenty-Eight

Ultimately, not everything can be told; it is a clear day in the middle of the spring, cold, the wind is like a knife, we walk through a small town, me and Saleem, on the way to my cousin's wedding, the streets are so crammed with cars that we abandoned ours at the edge of the town rather than negotiate the narrow streets.

We hear a din in the distance, a distinct hum that comes from the outskirts of the town. Without seeming to realise it he walks towards it, each stride increasing in length, bringing him nearer, so that he almost breaks into a run. I chase after him, tugging at his arm. Where are we going, the wedding is back that way. I point back the way we came, towards the cars that remain motionless, jammed together, horns blaring. Why are we going this way, why are we going towards that crowd. I just want to see what's happening, he says, we won't stay long. Other people are rushing in the same direction, towards the crowd and the noise, he keeps walking, pulling me behind him, and then we turn a corner and glimpse the crowd, a great heaving angry mass, armed with flags, a dull hissing noise emanating from them.

I think there is a protest, he says, I want to see what's happening, and I move with him again, submitting. He quickens his pace in tone with those moving around us, and soon we are jogging, dodging around people. Saleem, I say, I think we should turn back now. The crowd moves in unison, the police are hassled, shout into their radios, demanding reinforcements, there are people all around us now, and it is difficult to move. What's happening, he asks the man standing next to him. There's a new army base being built here, he shouts back through the clamour of the crowd, we are protesting against its construction. Let's go, I say, and tug at his sleeve, there will be trouble. I take a step backwards, trying desperately to retreat through the crowd that is surging forward, gripping his wrist in an attempt to tow him after me. People shout at the police, curse them, and some of them pick up stones.

Saleem begins to retreat, his eyes scanning the surrounding crowd. He sees a teenager, little more than a boy, cradling a rock between his hands, under his chin. The boy kicks out at a cat that weaves its way through the crowd, hair standing on end, anxious to find an escape from the stamping feet. He strikes the cat hard with his foot on its left flank, the cat flees, the boy holds the rock closer to his chin, he is watching a policeman. A group of soldiers have arrived on the scene, are parading along in front of the crowd, but the boy's eyes remain fixed on the policeman who is bellowing desperately into his radio. He watches the policeman, and Saleem notes that one of the soldiers is observing the boy. The crowd heaves forward, shouting something, we cannot hear the exact words of the chant, but it is about a homeland, the search for a home, it is an angry chant.

Saleem, I say, Saleem, let's go now, the wedding. I'm not staying here, I'm going. And I begin to turn from him. And then the boy makes his move, the boy with the rock cradled between his hands, with visible determination he manoeuvres the small rock so that it rests in his right hand, he tilts his hand backwards, slowly and with utter concentration, and the rock lies at an angle from his body. All the time he watches the policeman.

Before he can release the rock, transform it into an angry missile, Saleem springs towards him, for here on this frozen spring day, on this white chalk road that snakes downwards towards a distant valley, he sees this boy's life with such lucidity as if it were his own, he sees his life and what it will become if he throws the stone, the bleakness of his future if it meets his target, the darkness and the lack of hope, and the slow festering hatred inside him. He dives towards the boy, the energy and the madness of the people in this land, in this crowd, swelling through him as he leaps, reaching the boy a millisecond before the rock leaves his hand.

The boy looks at him, his mahogany eyes reading the intention in Saleem's, but it is too late and when he casts the rock he has lost his focus, so that it whistles past the policeman's left ear, before smashing onto the white road. Damn you, the boy curses at Saleem as he lands on him and they both tumble to the ground, the boy's nails pinching Saleem's back. But in the same moment a bullet is discharged, the roar of death in the sound is so very familiar to him, ringing out in the clear day, under the white sky that appears to have filled with snow, and the crowd is seized by panic, begins to disperse. The bullet sinks into Saleem's flesh, he remains on the ground, the boy wriggles out from under him, crazed with fear, abandons him on the street and disappears amongst the masses who are fleeing up the mountain road, back towards the village with the narrow streets and tall buildings where they can disappear into the shadows.

* * *

Some of them halt at a discreet distance, where they linger, shuffling their feet; others remain at the scene, screaming, panicked, but refusing to leave. In the dizziness of that moment you are aware of a great dart of ecstasy rushing through you as the boy escapes into the crowd, and disappears along the mountain road. He's escaped, you want to shout, for never in your life have you known such ecstasy. You have a heightened sense of awareness in those moments: Sahar is hysterical, screaming, and there is another voice, a man, pleading with her to calm down. They hover over you, their faces blurred, and other images too, from long ago – your mother's voice when you were young, the sunlit days of your childhood, the slap of the fishing line hitting the water, the thud of fish on a warm rock, the smell of the rosemary in the yard behind your home, the speckled metal of the junk Uncle Sabri collected there, and inside you the ardour for living that has always lived within soars to the surface, threatening to explode in a great rush of grief and desire; and you close your eyes for all that there is now is the eagerness in your heart to live, to refuse to succumb.

That is how you die: in the midst of an agitated fleeing mob, yet simultaneously in isolation, removed from everyone and everything, in complete and utter solitude you die, the face of your wife and a strange man hovering over you, quietly you creep from the world, it releases you, the world, with no questions, no recriminations, it simply lets you go, all is extinguished in that moment, everything that you are, and the girl knows it, the girl sees the life leave you, her hysteria intensifies, her screams grow louder and she beats at the soldier who stands by her side, and the soldier moves away from her in response to the orders of his supervisor, leaving her to kneel beside you until her screams become sobs and her breath becomes rakish and she clutches at her belly and moans in agony, and somebody shouts that she will need an ambulance first for the man is already dead.

Chapter Twenty-Nine

Do you know what a house is without him, she says.

She stares straight ahead at the clock on the wall. A tremble goes through her, starting in her shoulders and moving through her entire body, I watch it go through her. There are so many things, she says, there is the tree he planted last year on the balcony, where I like to sit in the morning and drink coffee. A miniature orange tree, she says. And there is the canary, she says, he used to release it from his cage and let it fly all around the house, until it would eventually tire and land on his shoulder. He liked when it landed on his shoulder, she says, he liked to sit with the canary on his shoulder. There are so many things, she says, there are so many things, there is nowhere to begin.

Her face is calm and still. Now you know, she says, that's how it was. That's how he died. Next week, she says, come, come next week. Please, come next week, Avi, please.

I hold the ticket in my hands, flicking it against the wood in front of me. Now you know, she says, now you know everything. Her eyes are dark, almost black. She raises her hand to her face and places one of her nails between her teeth.

Nobody ever quite understood what you were to each other, she says, but I did. From the beginning. You must help me, Avi. She looks right at me. Karim and I would live in the same house, she says, the home I shared with Saleem.

David is staring at her, a strange look in his eyes. It was cold that day, he says, she nods, he exhales the smoke, very cold, he says, colder almost than any day I remember, she nods again, she is rubbing her foot around the wet floor, creating designs out of the dirty splashes of water. The road was carved out of the mountain, David says, it was a steep hill, and there were crowds of people on it, and the wind that day was like a knife. She nods. Yes, she says, that's how it was.

We were called in, David says, the ferocity of the demonstration was completely unexpected. We were on our way to the territories. She doesn't move. He got in the way, David says, ran right into the riot. He shakes his head, he was foolish, he says, he didn't think, he got in the way, forgot to think like a soldier. She pushes her chair back, it screeches on the wet floor. I read later, he says, in the newspaper it said that he was a former soldier. It was a stupid mistake on his part, he says, unusual for someone who served. He stands up, sucks on his cigarette, eyes her through the gauze, not that I mean any disrespect to him, he just made a mistake, he says. Yes, she nods, and her eyes are closed and she is crying.

Zaki paces around in front of the open doorway, eventually he approaches. I gave you some extra time, he says, I gave you some extra time because she came late. He nods in her direction; her eyes are fixed on the ground, her finger remains between her lips. She stands to meet his gaze, I am ready, she says, I can leave now.

She turns to us, the rain on the roof is so loud that I cannot hear her words, but I see her mouth moving.

Next week, she says. I hold the ticket in my hands. There is the sound of a clap of thunder and the room darkens, her skin glows in the dim light, it is the colour of champagne.

The pregnant woman, David says, the baby, what became of them. She halts, turns again. Zaki reaches his arm towards her, a gesture that says she must leave now.

The woman went into premature labour, she says, she leans against the chair as if it is difficult for her to stand. The baby died, she says, the baby died before the emergency services arrived. David is rocking against the gauze, the cigarette is almost against his cheek. And the woman, he says. The woman, she says, the woman survived.

David begins to smoke again, though the cigarette is just a brown filter, he stares at her, it was cold that day, he says, it was so cold.

Zaki coughs, she turns to him, I will go, she says, I will leave now. I'm sorry they died, David says, I'm so sorry they died. She turns towards the doorway, Zaki walks behind her. At the doorway she raises her hand above her head, a gesture that suggests she believes it will shelter her from the torrential rain.

*

My father died on March 29th, 2001, one month after Saleem was shot. He died at dawn. He was making his morning meal: a roll he had taken from the dining room the day before, cheese, sliced cucumber and tomatoes. He was efficient as always; he didn't believe in a lingering breakfast; it was a purely functional meal. The morning was the most productive part of his day. He rose early, both in summer and winter, ate a brief breakfast, listened to the morning news, before beginning his work in the gardens. He would have watched the weather forecast the evening before and dressed suitably. It was always an immense relief to him, the predictability of the weather here.

When the heart attack struck, he had enough time to dial the emergency services, though he was dead on the kitchen floor by the time they arrived.

Gabi, the kibbutz director, came to my house on the kibbutz later that morning to break the news. I had moved home to recover after the bomb. I was on evening shift at the factory that week, and was reading the morning paper when he arrived. He had a natural air of authority and grace, and his voice was grave and heavy in keeping with the solemnity of the occasion. It was over in a matter of moments he said, they would all help me through my grief, I would have the full support of the community. It didn't make sense he said, a man still relatively young, who exercised regularly and spent so much time outdoors.

His involvement was a relief; he made the funeral arrangements in a quick and efficient manner that would have pleased my father, who despised all forms of time-wasting. The funeral itself was simple and unadorned, filled with kibbutz tradition. Gabi gave a speech, making reference to my father's service in the 1973 war, and how he had reared me alone after my mother left. This wasn't easy he said, but he always put his responsibilities as a father first. Everybody nodded in agreement.

After the funeral it came to me that I should clear the house of his belongings. He wouldn't want them left there taking up space that he no longer needed, for he was not a sentimental man. The air was still inside his home, the windows closed. A neat row of sliced tomatoes and cucumber lay on the chopping board in the kitchen, and the only sign of any discrepancy was the knife on the floor where he dropped it when the heart attack struck. His navy jacket was folded on the back of the chair and vivid images of him came to me: him standing straight in the gardens studying the plants, his eyes resting on each one, before deciding on his course of action for the day; his voice, naming them to me aloud, marigolds, sweet peas, sunflowers, explaining their preferences, what type of soil they liked, how much water they needed. His blue overalls, neatly ironed, creased down the middle, the smell of earth from his fingers. Him, sitting on the patio in the evenings, reading one of his books, raising his eyes to regard me from time to time, nodding with approval if he saw me studying from a book, frowning if he caught me staring into space. His peaked cap, his laugh, so abrupt, unexpected, so completely out of character. How he never left.

My father came to this country at the beginning of October 1973: he arrived at the kibbutz in the early afternoon, abandoned his rucksack on the steps outside the dining room and went to volunteer to fight in the Yom Kippur war. He was sent to the Egyptian front. His disappearance sparked a flurry of activity on the kibbutz, and there was much debate as to where he could have gone. Later, when asked to account for his actions, he never could, only that he was seized by a completely uncharacteristic moment of ecstasy and that the urge to go was immediate.

The war was hard for him, coming as he did from a northern climate, a man who once believed that the desert was filled just with sand, who only saw in the heady days of that October that the desert was not that at all, but actually stone, stone everywhere, rasping and cold and endless, the ground below him hard and the glaring sky above him endless and dead as the desert below. In the heat of the day, when his nostrils and throat were filled with sand and dust, he used to imagine that he was standing by the lake on a December evening. He breathed in the freezing air, and the sun no longer blinded him. And sometimes at night as loneliness crept all around him, surrounding him like a blanket, and the fear of the next day loomed before him, he imagined that he was home, for those lakes were home he confided in me once, and no amount of living anywhere else changed that; home is home, he said. Nothing he ever did in all of his life after could compare to the days of that October.

Afterwards he came back and continued with his life, rarely referring to it again. Sometimes when I was a boy he spoke about it in the evenings though he was not a talkative man. There were times when he would suddenly straighten himself, and a proud vacant look would enter his eyes. I grew to recognise these moments and I knew that October 1973 had made everything worthwhile for him. He told me once, on an evening in spring, when we sat outside in the twilight and the evening was heavy with the smell of the wallflowers that he so lovingly tended, reminding him for all of his life of his mother and their little garden in England, he told me there is always something you will remember as worthwhile.

The war seemed to remain recent in his mind with the passing of years, the suffering of the soldiers, their energy, courage, and endless ability to endure, the joy when it ended. And what's important to note, Avi, he said, is that a person can come to love any place at all, as long as there is anything worthwhile there. Take Sinai, he said, the sand and the stone, the heat of the days that almost cooked us alive, how we cursed it, yet I remember it fondly now. And he would laugh incredulously. And often I think of him in that place, surrounded by comrades who spoke a language he had not yet mastered, I think of him and of the army bases in the Sinai desert where he served, great conglomerations of concrete and iron thrown together on the desert rock, and of how he made his life there full, and how those neutral, passionless places became dear to him, sacred in his memory.

Chapter Thirty

July 24th, 2001

Avi Goldberg,
This is to notify you that you will present yourself at Camp 81 at 8:00 A.M. on November 4th, 2001. Your service will continue from November 4th through November 29th, 2001.

Chapter Thirty-One

March 16th, 2001

Dear Sareet,

I am writing to you from the darkness of a Galilee night ravaged by the winds, from the blackness that descends immediately before the first colours of the coming day appear in the sky; and from the depths of a deep exhaustion. I have not been sleeping well. There is a new housing development being constructed on kibbutz land (to be sold to private purchasers). The work being carried out at present, which appears to be a case of preparing individual sites, is deafening and lasts from daybreak through to nightfall, rendering an afternoon siesta impossible. In addition to this, the daytime noise seems to have seeped into the place, become an integral part of our lives, for the din continues in my head long after they leave each evening and before they commence work in the morning. Though perhaps it is not the noise at all that bothers me, rather the craze of uncontrolled capitalism that continues to spiral out of control on this kibbutz, not only among the kibbutz youth I might add, indeed some of the founding members have succumbed and have their names down to purchase a property. To me it is merely another element of a pattern I have watched develop for some years now, signalling the end of the ideology that brought me here. I am undecided as to whether or not it is a sign of failure, for life is change and is ever-moving, yet the prospect that perhaps the ideals we nursed in our pioneering days did indeed fail does continue to cause me some disquiet.

It is springtime again; hot, the Arabian winds are blowing from the desert, I have closed the shutters against their hateful mumbling, but their reach is long, relentless, they find a way to crawl inside, discarding layers of dust in their wake. Rain is forecast for tomorrow, but meanwhile it is hot and dry, the wind storms against the window, crashing at the shutters, and the cluster of pine trees outside creaks wearily under the constant assault, their needles are hurled about by the wind. Dust is everywhere, in my eyes, my throat, my lips are parched, it is futile, I cannot sleep.

I write under the assumption that you are calmer now than when I last heard from you, and have managed to place everything in perspective, accepted that I am not single-handedly to blame for everything to do with Avi, or with you and Avi, or with you, me and Avi, or even with your family in the Netherlands. Never mind if you have not, there will come a time when you will and I am not writing to discuss the past. We have scrutinised it separately over the years, ripped it apart, only to put it back together, each from our own perspective. One day we will make peace with it. I like to think that perhaps I have.

The reason I am in correspondence with you yet again is due to an event that occurred a couple of months ago, something perhaps insignificant but it has been playing on my mind nonetheless. I will get straight to the point: some time ago I brought Avi to a supermarket to carry out his weekly shopping. This was not a planned trip. Avi was still on crutches at the time (his body has since healed considerably and he has made incredible progress, it is remarkable to me how the flesh heals). As you know, he has returned to live here on a temporary basis, he has a small home on the other side of the kibbutz, where the younger people tend to live.

I had not intended travelling with him that day, he was meant to travel with somebody else, but in the end that person couldn't go. And as it happens I ran into him while I was out inspecting a new rose garden I am developing near the dining room that is proving to be quite problematic (greenfly were a major problem last year) and he mentioned he had intended going shopping but couldn't drive yet because of his leg. So I offered him a lift, and he accepted.

Avi expressed a wish to travel to a supermarket in one of those new shopping centres that have gained popularity here in recent years. I'm not sure that you spent enough time on your last visit here to notice them, or absorb such details of your surroundings, but I often think that you would not recognise this country should you spend any amount of time here at all. We were in the supermarket when a young man, an Arab, approached Avi and placed his hand on his shoulder. The young chap was smiling at Avi. We were walking towards the dairy section at the time. Avi seemed surprised when the Arab chap placed his hand on his shoulder, but he scarcely turned to the man before he was walking again, slowly, though it seemed he was familiar to him – he nodded at him. But the young man stopped dead for a moment as though surprised by Avi's reaction.

He recovered and began to walk along beside Avi. They chatted for a time and it was obvious that they knew each other. I hovered around them for where I come from it is normal to introduce people to each other, but Avi did not make an effort to introduce the young man to me, and I quickly realised that he did not intend to. They stood together chatting and for some reason I felt he was something to Avi, that he knew him, understood him, that they understood each other a great deal. I can't explain how I instinctively felt that, something about how they stood together, heads close, and how they parted as if there was more to be said than either of them could find the words for. Perhaps I am wrong, yet the incident continues to linger in my mind.

Of course there is nothing significant about that event – they could have known each other for many reasons, they could even have worked together here on this very kibbutz. There are plenty of Arabs employed in the factory here, and Avi worked there prior to his army service, and is indeed employed there at the moment.

But there is something else: I am sitting at the kitchen table and there is a photo of that young man in the newspaper in front of me. It is two weeks old, this newspaper, and it has been open on this page for the past two weeks, and I am sure it is him. I've looked at it many times, and often I walk away and remember that winter day in the supermarket, him touching Avi's shoulder, and I return to inspect the picture, and each time I become more certain it is him.

I've omitted to tell you the reason as to why there was a large photograph of him in one of our national newspapers. The thing is he was shot dead a little over two weeks ago, died immediately as it happens. His death occurred at some kind of a protest against us, the army or the founding of this state, or some such nonsense. They say that he was not engaged in an act of violence, that he intervened in an incident involving a young teenager (this is being thoroughly investigated) who himself was engaged in an act of violence against the IDF, and it seems that he was accidentally shot. All I can think is that he must have been involved in the violence in some way, given that he was shot and given that the army is extremely reluctant to shoot in any instance; but they say he had no criminal record and indeed served in our armed forces, which is not mandatory for his people by any means.

I have not spoken about this to Avi, nor have I seen much of him since this incident, though when I did he seemed somewhat withdrawn. I am not sure as to why I have written to you about this, only that the entire incident revealed to me that Avi, my son, is a mystery to me, a constant unsolved riddle, as much of an enigma as if I had abandoned him here and disappeared too. I don't know what he does in his free time, who his friends are, besides his peers here that he grew up with – what indeed makes him happy. I don't know what this man was to him, or how he knew him, or what his loss means, if anything at all. And this bothers me, Sareet, more than it should. Indeed it is highly possible that you know more of Avi from the monthly letters you receive from him, that by your leaving you came to know him in a way I never did in staying.

And something else. These thoughts brought back another, with an intensity for which I was not prepared – the time we first met on the steps of the dining room upon my return to the kibbutz after the war. You stood in front of me and there was something in you that I recognised immediately, and I knew then that the decision to come to this country had been the right one; but there was something more I saw in you then too, an inner hunger, a hunger that I was not entirely convinced I could satiate, even then, even after the war. I recognised it in you, and it both frightened and enchanted me at once, and the image of you that day has never left.

In one hour now, perhaps a little more, the racket that is the new building site they are creating here will resume again. But, for now, how deep the silence of the night – absolute, empty, so I find with a certain degree of surprise that I have lived again over the past few hours the days of those early summers I spent with you. And there is a constant image in my mind – a summer evening, you standing on the patio of our home facing a giant easel, the mountains of Galilee behind you shimmering in the evening light. You are painting a picture, a colourful affair full of light and flowers and beauty, you are smiling and there are splashes of paint in your hair. Avi sits near your feet, waving a stick at a stray cat that is enjoying the last rays of sunlight, his mouth is a round O and he is gurgling to himself – how enchanting everything about him was then.

I am walking through the door, home after a long day in the gardens, smelling of soil and geraniums and dust. You turn from your picture and smile, before turning away again, and in that moment I am all that there is for you, I see it in your eyes. There is a bottle of wine on the table and two glasses beside it and I sit there for a time and watch you paint, create an entire world of your own, a world full of colour and beauty. How mysterious that world you created was to me! That is the image.

Daniel

Chapter Thirty-Two

It is the end of the day, the light is beginning to fade, each prisoner prepares for the approaching night in his own way: some whisper to each other from their cells, others lie in the darkness listening to the raw voices around them, some write letters home, one prisoner gives a running commentary on what he thinks may be happening in a soccer match that is being played in Jerusalem this evening, his voice echoes through the darkness, obliterating the whispers of the other prisoners. Shut up, Moti, another prisoner says, shut up, okay, but Moti continues his tirade, and in the end we submit and listen wordlessly to his imaginary football game. The rain continues to fall, I peer through the bars at the gathering darkness. David is quiet, avoiding the door of his cell, I hear him shuffling about, turning the pages of a book; he doesn't speak.

I lie on my bed and sleep comes briefly, it descends upon me without warning, a goal has been scored in Moti's game, invoking much discussion among the inmates. When I awake the darkness is absolute, and the prison lies in utter silence, only the sounds of the night creatures break the solitude, the faint moonlight is weak on the leaves of the trees outside my window, and the wind moves about plucking them from the trees, flinging them around in the darkness. I sit at my desk, turn the page towards the glow from the candle; it is essential that I finish this before I leave here. I breathe in the odours of this late autumn night, and I begin to write.

*

There were weekends after he died when I returned to the beach, throughout the spring, and into the summer that followed, though it was hot then, and the spirit of him that seemed to exist there in the spring, a certain timelessness, evaporated into the heat of June and the scorching July that followed, so that sometimes when I went there I would decide not to return. But other times on a Friday evening it would call to me again, and I would drive there, through the dust and the stifling white brightness, past beaches packed with weekend visitors, boisterous camp areas. I would drive through the loud music, the glare and noise of summer, until I arrived, and it opened up to me like a kind of oasis. It remained deserted throughout that summer, the secret of its existence hidden from the holidaymakers.

In late July she came. It was a Saturday evening, I had been there for the weekend, the car was packed to leave. I was fishing, though with only half a heart to the task; the first fingers of inky darkness were spreading across the sky, though the black rock I sat on still held the heat of the day. A car sounded in the distance, his car, the sound of it was completely familiar to me. All time fell away, the car approached, nearer, nearer, spluttered to a halt, I turned, and she was standing there – Sahar. I stood on the black rock, and we regarded each other through the darkness that was swallowing the last remaining light from the evening sky.

For a moment, she said, for a moment it seemed you were him.

I moved my toe around on the rock, placed my hands in my pockets.

But then you turned, she said, but then you turned, and it could have been any beach and it wasn't him.

We stood there on the beach, she on the sand, I on the rock, and there was awkwardness between us. I've been coming here a lot, she said, I wondered if you come too. Her face was older, there were lines around her jaw, and her black eyes were hollow. Actually, she said, and she took a step towards me, I was hoping I'd find you here. I was beginning to think you don't come.

I come sometimes, I said. I came here this weekend just to think. I had a decision I needed to make. She watched me through the descending darkness, and her quietness, her very lack of reaction, the manner in which she was so similar to him at times, and moved so softly within her surrounding world, caused me to confide in her. I reached for my pocket and gave her the letter. She read the words, my words, stating that I was refusing to serve in the armed forces. She stared at the words for a long time and when she turned to me again there was something else in her eyes, and I knew that she understood how I had arrived at this decision.

Is it on account of him? she said. I shrugged, I don't know, I said, I only decided this weekend. Don't, she said. Her voice was harsh, raspish. Don't. But there was something calculating in her face.

I began to tidy up my fishing gear, I must go I said. I fumbled with the bait on the rock, gathered everything into a heap in the middle. What will it achieve, she said, what is there to achieve by doing it? She stumbled over the words. You would achieve nothing but trouble for yourself. I could barely see her in the darkness, only her shadow, her hair black against the profile of her face. He wouldn't want you to do this, she said, he wouldn't want you to bring trouble upon yourself. I shrugged. She bit down hard on her lip and I saw a bubble of blood glimmering before she licked it away. There is something else you could do, she said, there is something else. She moved nearer to the rock.

I sat on the rock and lit a cigarette. She crouched in front of me, stared over the lake, far away across the water distant lights shone. We didn't talk much, my mind was flooded with the possibilities of what she was thinking, and she seemed absorbed in her own thoughts, her eyes were distant and vacant. We sat like that for a long while, occasionally I rearranged my fishing tackle in the centre of the rock, or smoked a cigarette and listened to the echoes of the week-end holidaymakers coming to us across the water that lapped against the side of the rock like a timid creature. For some reason anything seemed possible that night. The air was heavy and filled with moisture so that I saw the sweat glistening on her face, and though we sat in silence for much of the time and gazed at the lake, an understanding grew between us just the same.

Later I addressed her again. I'm going to give them the letter, I said, I want to give it to them. They will arrest me. She looked at me. I will serve my time, I said.

They won't arrest you, she said, they can't. But then after a time she said, well, maybe they will.

Her words seemed to become absorbed in the night air

and she was silent again. Someone should be there with you when they come, she said eventually. You shouldn't be alone. And then, I will if you'd like, she said, I will be there when they come, if you tell me what day. She went to the car and wrote her number down on a small square of paper in neat writing, and then laughed suddenly, but of course you know our number, she said, well, my number, and then she blushed and was quiet again. I'll be there, she said. If you tell me when, I'll come. A mosquito hovered around her ear and she raised her hand to brush it away. She grew silent then, she didn't speak. I wanted to speak but whenever I stole a glance at her I saw that her face was twisted and raw with grief. After a time she moved again towards the car.

I must go, she said. I walked with her. There is something else you can do, she said. Avi, she said, Avi, you must promise you will give it some thought. When I ask, that is, when I ask just give it some thought. I looked away from the car, it depends what it is, I said. Don't go to prison, she said, there isn't the time. What do you mean, I said, what are you talking about? I moved closer to her, so close that I felt her breath against my cheek, and the impulse to move nearer, hold her against me, was there again, like the long ago day on the beach; but I recalled the grief that lived on her face just moments ago, the agony in her eyes, and I did not move towards her.

It will be November, I said, the beginning of November, that is when I am due for my service. Early November, she said, and her eyes were seized by panic, I thought it would be sooner. I reached my hand out and stroked her cheek, her skin was soft. Until when, she said, when will they release you? Late November, I said, November the twenty-ninth. They will release me when I have served for the time that I should have been in the Reserves. Those are the dates. That doesn't give me much time, she said. I lowered my hand. I thought she would speak again, reach her hand out to me, but she sat inside the car, reversed along the length of the beach, and drove away into the night, so that the sound of the engine became distant, until eventually it merged with the other sounds of the summer night, and the beach was empty again.

After she was gone an utter sense of desolation descended upon me, and I slept in the end, a tired hopeless sleep disturbed always by absurd dreams, so that when I awoke my neck was stiff, and my back ached, and I lay awake in the darkness recalling her eyes, the cunning that entered them, the knowledge they contained of what I had lost, I remembered the gleam in them, obscure, a flickering sense of desperation just beneath the surface, hidden deep in the depths of her eyes, and I wondered what it was she wanted of me. Though I didn't sleep much, a sense of resolution descended upon me and I posted the letter on my journey home.

*

A jackal cries out in the night, he is alone, separated from his peers, the pack lets out a series of answering yelps, but the creature does not find them immediately, his cries continue to reverberate through the desert, growing louder as his sense of desperation deepens, his naked sense of abandonment is revealed to the desert night. Somewhere in the midst of the writing I rediscovered, here in the darkness of my cell, the stillness of the beach, and I feel it now with absolute lucidity: the cold water against my skin, the sound of a fish flipping on the ground, choking in the hot air, the smell of the sun-baked black rocks, the feel of the sand between my feet, the girl, the softness of her skin under my hand.

I write, and after a time I cease to write. I place my pen on the desk and I tidy the pages into a stack.

Chapter Thirty-Three

July 28th, 2001

To Whom It May Concern:

This is to state that I, Avi Goldberg, will be unable to be in attendance at Camp 81 at 8:00 A.M. on November 4th, 2001. Indeed I wish to notify you at this time that I refuse to serve beyond Israel's 1967 borders. If you cannot assure me that you can accept my position on this going forward, I will not be in attendance on this day. You will not hear from me again on this matter.

Avi Goldberg

Chapter Thirty-Four

I slide the cold omelette around my plate, a trail of oil glistens in its wake. I prod my fork against its rubber texture, there is a knot lodged in my stomach, it has been there all morning.

So will you go home, I say. Will you go home when you are finished here?

David raises his eyes to mine, a look of surprise across his face, no, he says, no. I won't go home, you heard what she said. He raises a forkful of omelette to his mouth, chews it methodically. Maybe she didn't mean it, I say. Maybe you can sort it out once you're done here. He shakes his head and his hair falls into his eyes. We've been together a long time, he says, she meant what she said. He moves a slice of cucumber around his plate with his fork. There is no doubt about it at all, he says, she meant it. He takes a delicate bite from the cucumber. So where will you go, Avi, he says. I shrug.

I've decided to go to Egypt for a time, he says. After I leave here. There's a place in the Sinai we used to go, Ruti and I, before we were married. I'll sit on a beach, probably won't do anything much, after that I don't know. You have to consider, he says, even if she allowed me to go home, there would be the same argument next year, and the year after that. He reaches for the plate of chopped cucumber and tomatoes that lies between us. I might go further into Africa, he says, or I might come back. I'll have to see. He raises a slice of tomato towards his mouth, pauses, points his knife at me. She wouldn't even read the leaflets, he says.

He looks at me then, his eyes full of intent beneath the curls that bounce over his forehead. I must give you my number, he says. He takes a pen from his pocket, gropes around for a blank sheet of paper, in the end he removes one of the leaflets from his pocket, the leaflet with the photo of the eleven-year-old boy, the boy who was shot in Ramallah for throwing stones.

He writes an address across the leaflet. Here is where I'll be, he says. If you need to come there. It's a small place, he says. There's a beach there, that's where I'll be for a while. He examines the words on the page, adds his mobile phone number. Call me sometime, he says. Whatever you decide, wherever you go. He rises to his feet. David, I say, don't you think you should try to fix things. He moves away from the table, carries his empty plate to the area where other prisoners stack plates and wash dishes, then shuffles out towards the garden, raising his hand in a final salute of farewell, and after he has gone, I walk to my cell, place the small amount of possessions I brought to this place in my rucksack, and report to Zaki, who unlocks a series of doors, then gates, and suddenly the blue sky looms before me. Zaki hovers in the shadows, raises his hand to cover his eyes from the sharp light, his arms move as he points out the direction I must take; you'll need to get the bus, he says, straight down there, about fifteen minutes. He grips my hand tight and shakes it, squeezing it hard between his great paws, then slams the door shut behind me.

The sun is already hot when I emerge from the prison, the muddy puddles of water from the night rain evaporating in the heat of the day. I walk through the sunshine, the silent walls of the prison looming behind me, gradually disappearing into the morning haze. The sun grows hotter, the pack on my back already a burden; after a time I pause and gaze in the direction where Zaki said the bus stops would be, but there is nothing in the distance, just the black road, the ochre hills, and the sky.

The nothingness of this place astounds me. There is nothing here – the desert creatures have retreated from the heat of the day, concealed beneath the great lumps of rock that are scattered about amidst the feeble clumps of grass. I continue to walk until eventually a Bedouin village is unveiled through the dust, far in the distance, beneath me, shimmering in the desert light.

*

I think about the day I arrived here as I walk, the burning heat of that day, the warm Arabian winds that blew, Sahar, and how she didn't come. In the beginning I didn't notice how late she was. For a time I was busy, packing my bag, sweeping the floor, bringing out the rubbish. I stood in the early November heat, sweating under my gabardine uniform. I watered the plants in the garden, water evaporating into the air even as it rushed from the pipe. It was midafternoon, an utterly useless time of the day to water plants.

When the phone rang I dropped the hose and ran to answer it, leaving the water to rush out in a swell around the roses before expanding to a puddle and moving on to the lawn where it became a stagnant pool.

She wasn't coming, she said. She felt tired.

I could see her standing in the coolness of her living room, the bowl of overripe fruit, the ventilator whirring above her head. The room was dark because she had closed the shutters against the low November sun. Her voice was calm. She had something to ask, she said, she believed I would help her, she needed to believe that. She was sorry she could not come right now but she would come to the prison. Next week, she said, I'll come next week though it would be far better if you never went there.

That's okay I said, because I felt her tiredness. But you must give things some consideration, she cautioned, as it is I don't have much time.

In the end it did not happen like I imagined it would. There was just me, the soldiers, the heat of the day, white sweat, black guns. They allowed me time to close the windows and shutters of my little home, shut the shadows into the room and the bright afternoon heat outside. To check that Father's cat was out, that his collar and bell were safe around his neck. They didn't comment when I ran my finger along the books on the shelf, threw the remains of the lilies in the bin, placed the empty vase into the sink, and when I was finished they turned away as I looked around and locked the door. I placed the key under the mat, scratched the cat's head while they waited for me in the jeep.

I sat in the back. We drove away, through Father's gardens, and I noticed how they had begun to sprout weeds, past the dogs that had accumulated around the dining room. I named their names in my head, these dogs, associating them with their owners who were gone from my life now. We drove slowly and I had time to note the bougainvillea, how shapeless it had become, unlike Father's vision. We passed the workers in the orchards. There was Moshe Cohen hovering above the trees in a machine, shouting down orders to Tali Levi, who ignored him, crouched down as she was, drinking from a sprinkler. The water was running up her face as she drank, and it looked to me like she was kissing it.

One of the soldiers, who sat on the passenger side – a Russian with piercing blue eyes – kept turning to face me. I met his gaze every time, and in the end he would turn away and stare out the window.

I wondered if Sahar was sleeping, and then the soldier turned suddenly and thrust a cigarette towards me. I recoiled, for no reason other than that I wasn't expecting it, but he didn't like it and his eyes turned cold. He offered it instead to the driver, who accepted it, opened his window and began to smoke.

The arid air rushed in and again I recoiled, this time from the heat. The Russian soldier turned to face me again.

You want a cigarette he asked, and I didn't answer immediately. He nudged it towards me again, this Russian soldier, this recent immigrant who knew nothing of this land, and I almost took it. I stared at my boots and I closed my eyes. Then I shook my head, not definitively, but he saw it and withdrew his hand. We drove through the white hills of Galilee, and the dust blew into my face so that I wished they would shut the windows, but they were smoking and talking and no longer noticed me.

In Haifa we parked outside a shop with Arabic writing on the outside. At the entrance the cool scent of mint tea came to me through the heat. They must have been there before because the Arab inside greeted them with a smile and seemed to know what they wanted before they ordered. They ate falafel and the Arab poured us glasses of mint tea. It was dark inside, the only light coming from the doorway and the flicker of a television screen in the corner. I accepted the glass of mint tea from the Arab, and sat staring at the television. We left after around fifteen minutes, the Arab clasping our hands in a firm shake, and waving off our jeep.

Later, when we came to the orange desert, I had a desire to speak to the soldiers. The white glare from the sky was hurting my eyes and the right words would not come; they slithered past, eluding me like a long-remembered fragrance that you can no longer name, so that sometimes here at night I try to find them, the right words, but still they won't come, even though they are inside me somewhere, if only I could find them.

Chapter Thirty-Five

I continue to walk through the gathering heat of the day, the desert dust blowing in my face, when suddenly a perfect line of bus stops is revealed to me, emerging through the haze – each red stop the same exact distance from the other.

A dark-skinned Bedouin boy sits under a large umbrella sweating under heavy jeans. I nod at him, examine the fruit he has arranged on a plastic stand in front of him: slices of watermelon, lychees, and mango. I point at the watermelon, pay him too much money and walk away as he begins to count the change. It is deliciously sweet. I turn to him again and select another piece, I gorge on the watermelon, the pink juice runs down my chin and I wipe it away with my sleeve. The boy smiles to himself, I see his smile, purchase another slice of watermelon, until eventually I can eat no more. I examine the row of bus stops before me, pace up and down and the sun becomes hotter, the many aspects of this autumn day flood my senses: the immensity of the road before me, the reckless freedom I have to choose what bus I take, the bright colour of the bougainvillea that is a magnificent purple backdrop to the line of red metal bus stops, the little lizard that basks in the sun on the low wall beside me – his lazy tongue darting across the surface of the wall from time to time, the Bedouin boy who has begun to rearrange the watermelons in a large oval shape, a line of sweat across his brown forehead.

I stand for a time beside the red metal pole that marks the Ben Gurion express. I imagine her waking this morning, packing lightly, daring only to bring the barest of her possessions, sitting beside her suitcase, giddy with the belief that I might be there, creeping out before sunrise, placing her baggage in the car, closing the boot in the still manner she has, turning the key in the lock and moving inside again. I see her standing at the canary's cage, feel the slow passage of time, the ticking clock behind her. There is much that she cannot bring – the photos must remain there in their frames, the pictures on the wall that she so loves, all must remain there – for no hint of alarm must be raised as she makes her long journey to Ben Gurion airport.

*

Three years after my mother left, almost to the day, I killed my first butterfly. It couldn't have suspected its fate, not then, for it landed on my hand, a red butterfly, resting perfectly still on my palm. Only its black antennae moved, sensing the air around it, searching for danger, moving incessantly, never faulting. I closed my hand around it, it struggled against me, too late, tighter, tighter, it became a pulp in the palm of my hand, a bruised mass of scarlet. I stared at the remains for a time, then buried it in the ground, near the spot where she liked to sit in the evenings, beneath the jasmine that she asked my father to grow.

*

I move along the line of bus stops, stand for a time at the stop for Beersheba; beyond it is Eilat and, further still, the

Sinai peninsula, the place where my father once fought. I stare into the vastness of the desert, examine the address that David gave me, raise my hand to touch my cheek that is already burning in the heat of the day.

Chapter Thirty-Six

March 26th, 2001

Dear Sareet,

A terrible exhaustion has been with me over the last ten days, it seems that there is no release from it. I did not go to work today, they will have noticed my absence of course, there is much work to be done, especially at this time of the year when the garden is readying itself for the glorious display it rewards us with each summer. Two days ago Gabi came to visit. I sensed immediately that there was a purpose to the call, and that it was not a mere courtesy on his part. He broached the subject delicately, as is his way. It seems that there have been murmurs of discontent among some of the more long-standing kibbutz members that I no longer have the physical capacity to maintain my position as kibbutz landscaper, and a number of younger men have put themselves forward for the role. I told him that this was not the case and that I am still capable of carrying out my duties, indeed the care of the gardens is a high priority for me. His very lack of reaction told me that it was painful for him to be the bearer of such news. So in the end, after a brief silence on my part, I agreed with a nod, and questioned him as to when he would like me to step down. He said that he would like me to step down at the end of next month, so I assured him that I would comply with his wishes. There is much to be done, as I'm sure you of all people will appreciate. I would like everything to be in order when it comes to handing the kibbutz gardens over to my predecessor at the end of next month. As soon as I manage to shake this fatigue, I will work away with a vengeance so that the gardens shall be ready for the hand-over at the end of April.

It is late now, I drifted off to sleep early but woke some time ago imagining that I was a child again. The cat woke me, the cat you adopted, he was crying to be released into the night. I lay there for a short time orientating myself to the darkness, the cat continuing to pace up and down by the door. I think I may have been feverish, for it seemed that my mother was in the corner of the room, and I felt a great rush of love, something that I do not remember feeling for my mother, though perhaps I did. My strongest memory is only my desire to escape from the drabness of the life she created for us. I thought of her peeling potatoes over the sink, her face heavy with tiredness, her stomach swollen, for in most of my memories she is expecting one of my siblings, stirring her thick soup over the stove, beads of sweat on her forehead. And then I remembered the cold sometimes, the cold in the mornings when I awoke, the sound of her downstairs, moving around the kitchen, the sound of the kettle being filled and placed on the old stove, the sound of her stoking it, the strong movements of her hands.

I see you reading this, a small glass of sherry before you, your smoky eyes half-closed, a cynical frown across your forehead. I will say what I have to say and leave you alone:

I am writing because for the last weeks that image of you painting has remained in my mind. It is often the case that, once resurrected, memories can refuse to dissipate, and I have carried the image of that evening with me since I last wrote to you. And how many associated memories that one recollection has triggered! I've been tempted over the past few days to wonder what might have happened had I complied with your wishes when you wrote, some years ago now, and expressed a desire to return. I've been tempted to believe that the desire alone to return would have been enough, that what we had was sufficient, and that perhaps had you come back the years in between would have fallen away into nothing, so that they did not matter anymore. Perhaps you were right, perhaps we could have lived as a family again, perhaps I was wrong to deny you that opportunity. For there is this: you painted a picture one night and when you turned to me you told me you loved me, without speaking, there were no words involved, but I knew absolutely that you loved me. You and I fell in love on the steps of a dining hall surrounded by the endless Galilee mountains, I was wearing a filthy soiled soldier's uniform, you an apron, and your hair was pulled back from your face, but some of it had fallen lose and tumbled into your grey eyes. It was December, winter, and there was some rain in the air, a very light rain, delicious after the desert dust, and you turned your face upwards so that you almost seemed to drink it.

If you are unable to come back now it is of no matter; indeed, if that is the case please excuse this letter as the ramblings that have emerged from the depths of a deep exhaustion I have never before experienced. And from the realisation as to how many moments of our life slip away because we cannot find the right words. I originally wrote to you because I know absolutely that it was important for Avi to find the right words in the supermarket that day. He didn't find them. Never mind: I never had much luck finding the right words at the right moment either. I've somehow managed to discover them inside me now, it was something of a struggle, but I found them and they are here somewhere in the midst of this garbled letter; if you can find them perhaps it's not too late. Will you come back, Sareet?

Daniel

Chapter Thirty-Seven

The bus to Ben Gurion airport weaves through desert roads, carved out of the yellow rock, curving through endless mountains, their outlines quiver in the noonday heat.

For a time I stare out the window, the sun throbs against my forehead, I absorb the mauve desert landscape, the forlorn shrubs that sprout amongst the rocky crevices, alive only because of their stubborn refusal to submit to the persistent white light that beats down on them all day throughout a summer that must seem endless, their ability to put down deep roots that somehow prevent them from being washed away in torrents of cloudy water when the autumn rain arrives.

There are not many passengers on the bus. There is a man on the other side of the aisle, his eyes are closed, his rotund stomach rises and falls and occasionally a snore escapes from his throat. In front of him there is a young woman with three children; one of the children, a boy, is crying and reaching towards an orange lollipop that a chubby toddler clutches in her hand, her face is sticky with sugar, the young woman searches in her bag for another lollipop. I know I have one somewhere, she says to the boy in a soothing voice, and at the same time tries to wipe the toddler's face with a tissue. The eldest child stands before them, leaning against a metal pole, staring out the window at the desert, his face a blank canvas, oblivious to his mother and the other children. Behind me there is a Bedouin woman, sweating under layers of black clothing; she cracks sunflower seeds between her teeth, removes the sodden shells from her mouth, places them on a white handkerchief that rests in an exact square on the seat beside her.

I flick through the pages that detail the scenes from Saleem's life and a sudden thought occurs to me: I am seized by an obscure desire, the notion that I can leave him here, here in the desert now, it is entirely up to me. I open the window a crack, the warm breeze caresses my face, I release the first page, it flutters through the air, floats in the breeze for a time, before finding a place to rest. My eyes glide over the next page, and then I reach to the window and it meets the same fate. One by one the pages disappear, soar towards the heavens for a glorious moment before faltering, then drift towards the ground, to remain forever in the desert under the sun, where they will be covered in dust, partly eaten by insects, until they gradually become grey with the passing of time, bleached words staring at the sky, part of this land, a testament to what we lost.

*

My mother knew a man once, before the Yom Kippur war changed her life forever. They grew up together on the kibbutz, were close from an early age, inseparable. People on the kibbutz often referred to them over the years, remember Sareet and Uri they would say, remember how they were always together, and they would smile and their eyes would take on a tender look. One week into the war Uri was declared missing in the Sinai desert. He never returned. She wrote to me about those days, how she waited for word of him, wandered the mountains around the kibbutz all through that October, devoured by grief, paced up and down amongst the lists of the dead they posted in the dining room, how sleep refused to come so that a crazed exhaustion descended upon her, and how later she watched other soldiers returning safely, how they were welcomed and duly honoured. Only Uri did not return, and eventually traces of him were removed or disappeared, and people stopped talking about him, that was the hardest part.

Later she met my father, recently returned from the war. They met on the steps of the dining room one day in late December, and she made an instant decision, she said, she made a decision to love again, or to try her very best to love again. There were many reasons she fell for him, she said, he was handsome and there was a kind of optimism about him in those days, he had so many ideas and plans for the future. She liked how he had left his past behind, how he just got up one day and left, travelled to a country he had only read about and made it his home. She liked how he never looked back. And, she said, he knew nothing about her, she was a mystery to him, and everyone on the kibbutz knew all about her, and she liked that he knew nothing. Things were never meant to turn out the way they did, she wrote, how was she to know that she wouldn't forget; that the memory of Uri, the way he moved, the sound of his voice, would never diminish for her, that her mind would refuse to forget. If I'd know that then, she wrote, I'd never have entered into what I did. And then she signed her name, posted the letter, and never mentioned him to me again.

I don't know if there was ever a time when I didn't know about Uri; long before she told me the details I knew of him, he was always there, ever-present in our lives. Sometimes she would stop what she was doing, and a strange look would enter her eyes. I came to recognise those moments and I understood without ever possessing the words – for after all I was just a child – that he was there for her then, in a ray of light, or the odour of dust, or an unexpected shower of rain, the smell of burning pine in autumn fires, the perfume of the July lilies and the summer jasmine she begged Father to plant on the patio. It had been there before me, their love, before Father and me, and I accepted it, drifted through it, existed perfectly and happily in the same world where she lived without him, understood her loneliness without ever knowing that she was lonely.

Eventually I came to believe that her life with my father and me was doomed long before she left that July day, for she understood something, my mother, about life, how very short it is; and how could my father have known that day, on the steps of the dining room, how could he have known in the face of her beauty that her mind would refuse to forget and that she would never let go.

*

I continue to discard the pages from the window. The Bedouin woman behind me has noticed, she leans forward, places the sunflower seeds beside the white handkerchief and presses her oily wrinkled face up against the window as the pages drift through the air. The bus snakes through a banana grove, one of the pages is entangled in the branches, and a short burst of laughter escapes from her.

She looks at me and her eyes dance.

It is liberating. I cannot know where each page will settle, if someone will one day come upon it, hold it in their hands, touch the child, Saleem, his lost mother, for just an instant. There is emptiness too as each page, each word, is sucked into the desert, abandoned to choke forever under layers of dust in this land burdened under the weight of time and history. For words, after all, are things full of life, humanity, and after the last page flutters from the window a void descends, and I sink back, exhausted.

A town looms in the distance, buildings black against the bright horizon, the desert is coming to an end, the terrain becomes less inhospitable and more plants grow among the stones, the mountains fade away into the distance. Soon the immensity of the sky will diminish, and we will reach the city, and eventually the airport. We stop at a bus stop and a group of teenagers board the bus, pushing against each other in a bid to reach the rear-end first.

*

My mother left in July. Father told me a little about that day, years later, that it was hot, the hottest day that year. When she woke that morning she cried and begged him to take her to England. He explained to her that he could not leave because there was work to be done on the kibbutz where they lived, and he believed in that work and in the future, not just for him he said, but for the country, for future generations.

It's not about individual happiness, he said. It's about the collective happiness of the community. You must remember that.

And with those words we became the inbetween people, Father and I, the people who were left behind, condemned to live only with the memory of her, days that contained the possibility of stumbling, however blindly, into her, so that once the smell of paint drying on an easel brought her back to me so completely that I believed for a moment she had never left, and another time the smell of freshly cut geraniums in a vase on a table gave her back to me again in such reality that I had to turn away so that people could not glimpse my face; and if I lived my entire childhood anticipating such moments, I never hated her for leaving, nor did I ever question why I waited, or why the belief that she would one day return occasionally surged through me.

*

A black cloud storms towards the sun, descending on us from the city that looms dark before us, and suddenly it is raining, the bus slows, the driver leans forward, peering through the windows, in a vain attempt to see the black road before him, and in minutes there are great driving torrents of water moving across the arid ground. The road glitters black with rain, the drops fall like tiny yellow diamonds trapped in the sharp light from the headlights of the bus. A sadness I did not anticipate has descended upon me. Until now I'd supposed that, like my father, I could simply leave without looking back. I think about Sahar, and the hours and days ahead, how she will turn to me when she sees me. I wonder about her and her leaving, for she understands nothing about it, she understands nothing about the blackness of leaving.

The rain continues to fall, but now a finger of light escapes through the barrier of clouds, breaking through and descending on the wet ground before us, and suddenly we are in the town. The fat man opposite me does not awake despite the sudden burst of light, the Bedouin woman continues to snap sunflower seeds between her teeth, the weary mother bounces the toddler up and down on her knee, strokes the face of the sleeping boy beside her. The group of teenagers chat among themselves, their laughter vibrating throughout the bus. We drive through the finger of light, the bus becomes bright, the light changes and the face of each passenger glows. Only the child sees it, the boy who still stands, leaning against a metal pole, staring out the window, he glimpses the finger of light, and he stands up straighter, in a resolute manner, and his back becomes stronger. The clouds cover the light again, and it dims, the bus grows darker, but he continues to stand erect, and after a moment he lets out a gasp, collapses into his allocated seat and holds his younger sleeping brother against him.

First published in Great Britain by:

Ashgrove Publishing

an imprint of:

Hollydata Publishers Ltd
27 John Street
London WC1N 2BX

by arrangement with:

The Permanent Press
4170 Noyac Road
Sag Harbor, NY 11963
USA

© Emma McEvoy, 2012

The right of Emma McEvoy to be identified as the author of this work has been asserted by her in accordance with the Copyright Designs and Patents Act 1988.

No part of this publication may be reproduced, stored in a retrieval system or transmitted, in any form or by any means, electronic, mechanical, photocopying, recording or otherwise, without the prior permission of the publisher.

ISBN 978 185398 172 2

First Edition

Printed and bound in England